HOW TO SHOP LIKE A LOCAL

Le Shop Guide

CHLOE QUIGLEY
& DANIEL POLLOCK

We met in 2000 while freelancing at a Melbourne advertising agency. More interested in talking about the weather, clothes and careers we could do from the swimming pool, we decided to create Michi Girl. Since then we have written thousands of daily fashion forecasts and three books: *Like I Give a Frock*, *What on Earth Are You Wearing?* and *Le Shop Guide*. Today we have our own creative agencies, Ortolan (Chloe) and Jane (Daniel). We still prefer to work from the pool.

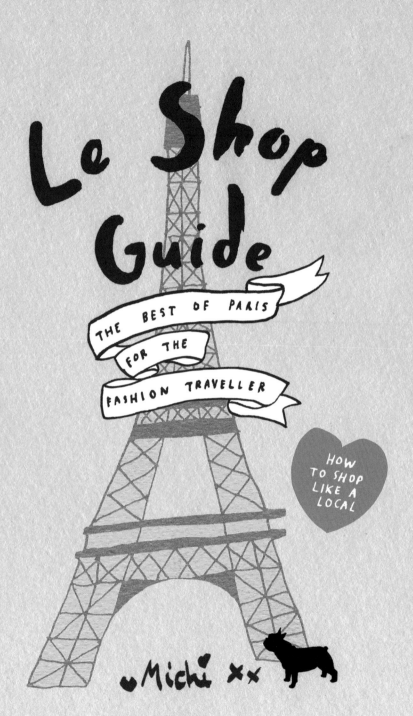

Le Shop Guide

THE BEST OF PARIS FOR THE FASHION TRAVELLER

HOW TO SHOP LIKE A LOCAL

♥Michi xx

VIKING
an imprint of
PENGUIN BOOKS

Contents

INTRODUCTION

LE GUIDE FOR
THE FASHION TRAVELLER. 1

HOW TO USE LE GUIDE. 4

MY HELPFUL SHOPPING CATEGORIES. 5

LE PLANNING

WHEN TO GO. 8

PACKING FOR PARIS. 10

SLEEPING. 12

BEFORE YOU GO. 16

LE SHOPPING

OPENING HOURS. 21

CURRENCY AND MONEY. 22

THE ONLINE ROULETTE. 13

LE GETTING AROUND

TAXI, BICYCLE, METRO,
BUS, WALKING. 24

DEPARTMENT STORES 28

TUILERIES GARDENS 36
Le Lovers' day 54

LE PALAIS ROYAL 66
Le good times day 84

ABOVE HÔTEL DE VILLE 90
Le free day 98

CANAL SAINT-MARTIN 110
Le posh day 120

LE MARAIS 130
Le postcard day 164

SAINT-GERMAIN-DES-PRÉS . . . 168
Le tiny day 178

FLEA MARKETS 190

SHOPPING CATEGORIES 204

INDEX 206

Introduction

When I was little, my mum had this thing called 'The Catastrophe Scale'. It was her way of illustrating that my major meltdowns were diminutive in relation to the real catastrophes of life. For instance, a tutu being in the wash is not on the same scale as finding you were born with a tail. You could argue that clothes are not that important, but no one can argue that Paris is the best place in the world to shop. Whether you need couture, cheap and chic or vintage gems, Paris will solve your problems. This book is your answer to finding what you need (want) and where to find it. I hear they have quite good coccyx surgeons too.

At the risk of offending the other quarter of a million cities in the world, Paris is the best city ever. Yes, there are lots of museums, art galleries, bridges, churches, and of course that big tower. They are all old and very, very important but there are plenty of other books and a world of Google to cover those. This book is for one thing and one thing only – SHOPPING.

Paris and shopping go hand in hand. Or better still hand in vintage Dior glove (*see* Catherine B page 176). Fashion was invented here. Sure, Napoleon didn't do us any favours by popularising three-quarter length pants in the eighteenth century but, apart from that, Paris has been responsible for giving the fashion traveller a reason to visit for hundreds of years. Chanel, Dior, Balenciaga, Hermès, Yves Saint Laurent and Louis Vuitton all helped shape 'the city of the light wallet' we know today. But any tourist with a credit card can shop their way through the obvious. I'm here for the other shops. The ones that will help you look, act and shop like a local, no matter what your budget or taste (well, it's mainly my taste but I'm the one writing the book so I must know what I'm talking about, right?).

17. BATIGNOLLE
MONCEAU

16. PASSY

15. VAUGIRARD

LES
CHAPTERS

1 TUILERIES GARDENS
2 PALAIS ROYAL
3 HÔTEL DE VILLE
4 CANAL SAINT MARTIN
5 LE MARAIS
6 SAINT-GERMAIN-
   DES-PRÉS

ARRONDISSEMENTS

18. BUTTE MONTMARTE

19. BUTTES CHAUMONT

9. OPÉRA

10. ENCLOS ST LAURENT

4

ÉLYSÉE

1

2. BOURSE

20. MÉNILMONTANT

1. LOUVRE

2

3. TEMPLE

5

11. POPINCOURT

3

PALAIS BOURBON

6

4. HÔTEL DE VILLE

6. LUXEMBOURG

5. PANTHÉON

12. REUILLY

14. OBSERVATOIRE

13. GOBELINS

HOW TO USE LE GUIDE

Paris is officially broken down into arrondissements. These are areas, numbered one to twenty, spiralling out from the middle of Paris, on the right bank of the Seine, in a clockwise direction. Think snail. (Cute? Now think about eating one... sorry but it's Paris and you really should try it once. It's just like eating chewy garlic butter, but with a shell.) But I digress. Arrondissements are famous and everyone identifies where they live by this system. 'I am Pierre, I smoke and paint and live in the 3rd.' 'Shall I bring some macarons to dinner? I live in the 2nd and don't have far to go, shall I swing by Ladurée?' You get the idea.

However, they don't really help me in my shopping travails so I have left them out. Rather, I have mapped the shops I love the most, put them in groups so you have shopping clusters all over town. I have invented my own areas (oh the arrogance!) based on Metro stations or places that are too big to be ignored (gardens, squares, towers, stuff like that) or just because I wanted to (and sometimes it's better not to ask me why). As a special treat, I have also included some places to rest – shopping can take it out of a girl. You'll need a pit stop every now and then to watch the Frenchies go by and plan the rest of your day. Take it from me, there is nothing like people-watching in Paris.

MY HELPFUL SHOPPING CATEGORIES

Now for the important part – the shops.

 With the help of my very fashionable local friends I have put together a list of 100% Pure Paris Shopping Gold. Sniff the book. Can you smell that? That's the scent of the best department stores, independents, vintage, affordable chic, and budget blowing shops in all of Paris. That other smell is a croissant and a cigarette. Sorry.

 I have personally vetted each and every one of these stores for your shopping pleasure. You can choose how to use this information – it could take you four weeks to get through it all, it could take you four days to visit just a few gems. You may wish to shop by map, or you can go straight to the summarised categories in the index. These categories have been thought out to best solve most shopping emergencies. Should you need to buy an outfit with your last few euro, a quick stitch and button moved to make room for more quiche, or a present to take home to ensure everyone knows you have just been to Paris, here is your guide:

Affordable chic
Looking like Paris without paying through your Eiffel Tower can be tough if you don't know where to go. I am here to help you sniff out style without having to sell your passport to a pimp.

Blow it
The budget that is. This section delivers upscale alternatives to Chanel (without necessarily saving, to be honest). Some beauties if you are feeling fancy.

Très French
Gifts that scream 'I've been to Paris' are vital, to scream to your friends and family 'I've been to Paris!'. Whether the gifts are to appease their jealousy or assuage your guilt, or just to suck up, these shops will have you sorted.

Cheap and cheerful
Budget fashion, Paris-style can be a thing of beauty. The only thing better than the adrenaline rush of spending a fortune on clothes, is saving a fortune and still looking like a million bucks.

Shoes, bags, dog collars
No explanation required really. These shops have leather bits. And yes, that includes dog collars. And no, not the kind you are thinking. Get your head out of the gutter and your tootsies into a killer heel.

The cool gang
You can't go wrong with these pearlers. There is barely a garment here that would be deemed passé by anyone, so if you're drunk or simply don't trust your own taste, you are in good hands with this lot. You'll look like you just stepped out of the not too distant fashion future.

Paris vintage
They make a meal outta vintage in this town. It's a serious business. I imagine all the big-deal traders scheming behind each other's backs to get the best deceased estates – slashing tyres and faking addresses, that kind of thing. Their obsession for trash is our pleasured treasure.

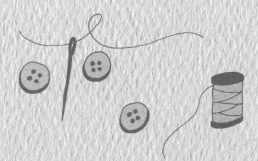

Look at me!

Inspirational retail spaces, even if you don't buy anything, are worth a visit if for nothing else but eye candy. Brilliant design, great visual merchandising, interesting layout – all still good for the soul even if it doesn't have a happy purchase ending.

French knickers

It's what's underneath that counts for French women. You can see in their confident stride that they are wearing great lingerie. What's more, they are not wearing it for a man, they are doing for themselves. Well, so they say.

Pampered Paris

Hair, nails, fragrance. These places are perhaps not the first thing you think of when you're away from home, but pampering Paris-style is pretty sweet. And as this is the land of the fragrance, you can't leave Paris smelling the same as when you arrived.

The Help

Tailors, alterations, drycleaners. All handy in Paris. It may be that all the smoking you have taken up drops some weight. Or it could be that all the croissants you have taken up add a little. Or, the best of all, it may be that you find the greatest vintage Dior dress of all time but it just happens to be a teeny bit big.

Last minute gold

A cluster of cool shops on the way to the airport is a must. It's pretty dangerous, as if you have any space on your Visa card you won't shortly. I once bought a Marni skirt for a month's pay on the way to the airport … bad choices, good times!

Sit and sip

Shopping is hard. Take a seat. Look around. Drink wine. They say that Parisians never drink alcohol during the day – it is very passé. But hey, you're not Parisian are you?

Le Planning

Spring: March–May

Of course everyone wants to go to Paris in the springtime. There are daffodils in the Jardin du Palais Royal, you can wear bare legs and order a pizza to be delivered to you on the banks of Canal Saint-Martin (pinkflamingopizza.com). It's the cliché – colourful, poetic, frisky Parisians. However, there is also a trillion other frisky tourists and bad hay fever to take into consideration. You'll need to weigh up higher prices and long queues against boozy nights with cheery locals. It's a tough one.

Summer: June–August

Generally j'adore summer best of all the seasons but in Paris there is a key ingredient missing in summer: Parisians. All the little, cute independent shops close and locals hightail it out of town. If you want to be hot and sweaty with a bunch of other foreigners be my guest, but if you're looking to fall in love with a local, you'll have to go some other time. For that matter, if you are there to do a little business you can forget it – Parisians don't do work in summer, they just don't. The city has a metaphorical 'gone fishin' sign on the gate. That said, there are free parties and lots to do as the town hall desperately tries to hold on to tourism. Maybe if you are into French shopping but not so into the French, it's your season.

Autumn: September–November

Paris is lovely in autumn (fall, whatevs). It's just after the long summer break so energy is high and it's all go, go, go. It's the start of low season too so the flights are a frac cheaper and, of course, the trees are very pretty. Even better, it's that great season where we get to add the 'trans' before the season. For me it's the exciting start of a new wardrobe – layering, a light scarf, jeans instead of legs out, a hat peut-être, sandals swapped for ballets. Ooh I love an autumn wardrobe! Remember, it tends to get very cool towards the end of the season and Parisians are prone to Seasonal Affective Disorder, so perhaps treat them respectfully. It's hard to be so perfect all the time after all.

Winter: December–February

Strange things happen in winter. The autumn gloom has really set in but then, presto, the city finds her festive mood and gets her yah-yahs out for Christmas. The lights come on, the red wine is aplenty and romance can blossom. Unless of course you are like me and despise the cold. But, if you can hack it, the city is almost magical it has so many lights a-blazing. Clothes are a slight issue, with a definite need for a really warm coat that you are happy to wear every day. Being in and out of heating means it's a constant strip tease, so be sure to layer up. In, out, off, on … Sounds saucy, it's not. It's annoying. But it's Paris, so who cares. The air is clear and crisp, you don't sweat as much on your bike. See, I can find the silver lining in anything!

Fashion Weeks: March and October

Either a good reason to come or a good reason to stay away, depending on your point of view. March and October make for a flurry of flesh as the streets become runways of their own. Go sit in the Tuileries Gardens for a day and be mistaken for a blogger. Ok, so maybe no one will actually be looking at you, but still …

PACKING FOR PARIS

It would be unrealistic of me to tell anyone what to pack for a holiday. Firstly, in the words of Coco Chanel, fashion is made to become unfashionable, so by the time you read this it's potentially out of date. And secondly, what do I know about what you want to wear? So let me give you the advice I wish I had been given the first time I went to Paris. Look as good as you possibly can at all times but be yourself. If being yourself is dressing like a two bit whore, maybe Paris isn't for you. But confidence is vital.

Parisian women look like they own the joint. No skulking around looking self-conscious and overproduced. Natural hair, bare-looking face, timeless pieces and an attitude to burn and you'll be fine.

If you're really so unsure of your own taste and need me to tell you what to pack, then here is a tip: lots of black, ballet flats and killer accessories. A good scarf, a blazer, and pair of Converse for all the walking you'll do shopping for more shoes. Just look like you don't have a care in the world and you'll fit right in. Statement jewellery is a great thing to travel with. That way you can wear black all the time, but have one great Karen Walker costume necklace and you're good to go anywhere.

On a practical level, winter really is cold but there is so much to see that you won't want to sit around indoors, so you'll need to be prepared. I recommend thermals. They are not like your nana used to wear – you can get a little merino thermal singlet or tee and it will be your best friend. Like your Nancy Ganz, no one will know it is there but you'll feel much better for it! As I already mentioned, you really will need a good, warm coat. Puffers are de rigueur in Paris. I am not a fan, preferring a classic wool coat, but they are so heavy. For travelling you can't go past a puffer – they squish to nothing and are not so bad really. Try Moncler to avoid looking like a backpacker. (Last time I went I bought a coat on sale and after lugging it around every single day, I hated the sight of it so much I left it behind. If you happen to find a navy wool hooded overcoat in a cupboard in Le Marais, be my guest!)

You'll need warm, wool socks. None of this cotton rubbish – if it's -5° at thermometer height, it's half that on the footpath. You'll need a hat too, as much as I hate to say it. You all know I hate a hat, but you also know 80% of your body heat is lost through your head, so get over that vanity and wear a beanie (easy to be wise after the event, I have a chunk missing from getting frostbite on my ears).

The other months are easier. Layers, your favourite things, lots of black, great accessories to mix it up. And let's face it, you are here to shop, so take less, buy more. 'Oh drats, I accidentally forgot, well, clothes. Silly me, I'll have to start again. What a shame.'

Ideally you have a French lover you can hook up with in Paris and don't need to worry about accommodation. If this isn't the case, then you're going to need to allocate some important shopping money to accommodation. Bummer. Depending on the length of your stay (and depth of your wallet) there are two important questions you need to ask yourself: Which area do I want to stay in? And, Do I want to eat out every day? If you want to position yourself in the heart of the shopping action, then the Marais is your best bet. There are a lot of small hotels and apartments available for short stays. I prefer the apartment option as I like to make my own breakfast and pretend I'm a local. However, if you want the full Paris postcard experience you might want to choose somewhere more scenic like Saint-Germain. If you don't want to Google your life away here's a small selection of my favourites:

APARTMENTS:

3 Rooms Alaïa
5 rue de Moussy
75004 Paris
Tel: +33 1 44 78 92 00

Seeing Paris through my eyes is pretty amazing I know. But just in case you want to swap my eyes for something more, well, French-Tunisian, I thought you might like to try this apartment by Tunisian-born designer Azzedine Alaïa. Designed to feel like a 'home from home', 3 Rooms Alaïa consists of three (obviously) modern self-contained apartments inside a seventeenth-century building. Chic, spacious, and smack bang in the middle of the Marais.

Airbnb
airbnb.com

If you're looking for cheap and cheerful apartments (or even bed and breakfast) this is a good site that hooks you up directly to owners.

Herouet Apartment
40 rue des Francs-Bourgeois
75003 Paris
Tel: +44 207 688 0531
www.city-apartments.org

Imagine a French Melrose Place. Ok, now swap Billy and Alison for Pierre and Gigi. In the heart of the Marais, these chic apartments have everything you could want in a Paris home: beautiful exposed beams with floor to ceiling windows, kitchen, two double bedrooms, two bathrooms, wi-fi and a film library if you want to stay in for the day. This would make Amanda jealous for sure. (If you're not following my *Melrose Place* references by now you are dead to me.)

Paris Attitude
parisattitude.com

Daggy name but thousands of apartments to choose from covering all budgets. They also have long-term rentals if you're lucky enough to be staying longer.

HOTELS:

Hotel Le Crayon

25 rue du Bouloi
75001 Paris
Tel: +33 1 42 36 54 19
www.hotelcrayon.com

Any hotel that encourages you to draw on the walls is either insane or really fun. Either way, they are friends of mine. Julie Gauthron and Christophe Sauvage have scoured antique shops and flea markets around Paris to furnish the 27 rooms of this handcrafted hotel. The Louvre Museum, Printemps and Galeries Lafayette are all within walking distance.

Four Seasons George V Paris

31 avenue George V
75008 Paris
Tel: +33 1 49 52 70 06
www.fourseasons.com/paris

Four Seasons George V is one of the hotels that you should all try to stay in before you die. It is so expensive and such a once-in-a-lifetime experience that there is only one way to stay there – the same way I did. Years ago while I was travelling in Europe, my dad had to go to Paris on business so we decided to meet there. He was foolish enough to leave the hotel bookings to me. It wasn't until I ran into Prince Charles in the foyer that I realised the magnitude of my brashness, but hey, you only live once. It might as well include a few days with 9000 fresh flowers a week, a Hermès fitted-out Rolls Royce and a world class spa, don't you think?

Mama Shelter
109 rue de Bagnolet
75020 Paris
Tel: +33 1 43 48 48 48
www.mamashelter.com

Excellent name and individually designed rooms by
Phillippe Starck make Michi love Mama. Situated in the
'diverse' (out of the way) 20th arrondissement, this is a great
(and surprisingly cheap) hotel if you don't mind the travel.
The really helpful and well-designed website will give you
confidence that they know what they are doing.

Hôtel Le Bellechasse
8 rue de Bellechasse
75007 Paris
Tel: +33 1 45 50 22 31
www.lebellechasse.com

Fancy a Christian Lacroix art-directed hotel room? Just
around the corner from the Musée d'Orsay in the beautiful
Saint-Germain district, Hôtel Bellechasse is part of the
Small Luxury Hotels of the World family. Individual rooms
with wallpaper featuring butterflies and posh Edwardian
gentlemen. Finally, together at last!

MICHI

BEFORE YOU GO

While I'm all for jumping on a plane and flying by the seat of my Rag and Bone jeans (perfect for flying — feel like leggings, look like jeans), there are some things in Paris you need to plan before you leave. Usually I find planning quite boring, but eating in every night because you can't get a restaurant booking is way more boring, trust me. And wasting time at the airport feeling lost is equally mind-numbing. Pre-production is vital, friends, albeit not that sexy.

FOR YOUR ARRIVAL

First impressions count for everything and I personally like the idea of everyone in Paris thinking I'm way more important than I really am. For only 10 euro more than a cab, please book a private car service to pick you up. Not only do you get to see a dude hold up your name on a sign, it beats the hell out of lining up with all the other suckers waiting for a cab at 5am. Be sure to book a week before you plan to arrive. Try G7 Taxi Service: www.g7taxis.fr

Note: If you arrive in peak times I'd avoid taking a car of any description. You'll spend hours in traffic with a smoking driver and world of rage. I'd just suck it up and catch the RER B train from Charles de Gaulle — a speedy but stinky 30-minute ride to the centre. At least things will only ever get better after that.

DINNER RESERVATIONS

Like anything good in life, getting a table at a great Paris restaurant requires consideration. In my opinion, it's what you wear not what you eat that counts, but where you eat should be resolved ahead of time. If you book before you leave home then all you'll need to worry about is planning your outfit. Two of my favourites are Derrière and Le Châteaubriand.

Derrière
69 rue des Gravilliers
75003 Paris
Tel: +33 1 44 61 91 95

Book in advance at www.derriere-resto.com.

Le Châteaubriand
129 avenue Parmentier
75011 Paris
Tel: +33 1 43 57 45 95

Le Châteaubriand is a must. The menu changes every night depending on the market day the chef has had, so you can go back as many times as you like (or can afford) without getting bored. The building is an old 1730s bistro near the Bastille so you'll really feel a French connection.

EIFFEL TOWER QUEUE JUMPING

Don't even think about not going up the Eiffel Tower. Yes it's touristy and surrounded by pickpockets and 10-euro baguettes, but it's the Eiffel Tower! The best advice that I can give you (apart from the rest of this book) is to book your ticket before you leave. Just remember to keep your sunglasses on to avoid eye contact with those poor suckers lining up for hours as you scoot past them. Less line time. More shop time! Buy your Eiffel Tower ticket online at www.eiffel-tower.com.

DAMAGE CONTROL

Nothing repairs the damage of a long-haul flight like fancy new hair and nails. Manucurist is reputedly one of the best manicure salons in Paris. I say reputedly as I have never actually been able to get an appointment. I wish I had me to remind myself to book next time.

Manucurist
13 rue de la Chaussée d'Antin
75009 Paris
Tel: +33 1 47 03 37 33
Open: *Monday–Saturday*
10am–7pm,
until 9pm on Thursday
Closed: *Sunday*
Metro: *Chaussée d'Antin – La Fayette*
www.manucurist.com

And another thing…
Try not to land on a Sunday if you want to hit the ground running. Shopping is non-existent (apart from the Marais) and food is hard to find. I learnt this the hard way. Twenty-six hours of travel and no food to be had was pretty ugly, trust me.

Le Shopping

Shops open from Monday to Saturday between 10am and 7pm. In true up-yours-I-deserve-a-day-off style, barely anything is open on Sunday. If you are twitching for a fix, head to the Marais where you can get some action in the afternoon. Louis Vuitton and other shops on the Champs-Élysées have also defied this rule and swing their doors open on Sundays, but who can afford them?! The Marais will never fail to please with a parade of hipsters on a Sunday and a happy feeling in the streets – no cars allowed on Sundays so it's just lots of bikes and feet down the middle of the road and smiles all around.

SALES

The big ones (global financial crises aside) are in January and July. So, by my calculations, there is no month that we can get the best weather *and* cheapest clothes *and* the friskiest locals. C'est la vie. Come February and August however, plenty of shops still have a sneaky sale rack up the back. Being generally understated as a city, they don't like to flaunt the crap stuff so you might need to search for it. I really admire their restraint – nothing like home where it's constant discount upon discount. The French are positively frigid compared to the pimping retailers in other cities, so enjoy the search. You'll be glad for it. We always value things more when they don't come easy.

I wish I could say that the money is francs – it sounds so much cuter. I'm going to France to spend my francs... But like the rest of the European Union, France is ruled by the Euro. It's pretty – the coins mix silver and gold which is really cute and the notes are in a spectrum of colours. It's so nice. Does that help? No? Ok, let me try something else. A coffee will cost you €3 and a beer about €7. I guess dealing in drinks is a lot easier.

A bit about VAT

If you're not good with tax forms and don't plan on spending up that much then maybe skip this bit. But for those of you who take pleasure in getting some cash back from the poor French government – this is for you.

If you spend a minimum of €175 in the same store on the same day you are eligible for the *detaxe* (VAT) refund. If you're shopping with a friend this is a good time to pool resources and share the tax refund love. Also good for department store shopping like Galeries Lafayette, Printemps and my favourite, Merci. Ask for a form before you leave the store and remember to keep your receipts. At the airport on your departure, you will need to provide your ticket, passport and the forms that you have collected during your shopping. Once Customs has reviewed everything, they will endorse the copies and then you just need to pop them in the mail before you jet off. It takes a while for the refund to come through, so be patient, they are probably just out the back having a fag. If you haven't received your refund within a couple of months contact the store(s) where you made the purchase, not French Customs.

LE ONLINE ROULETTE

To tell you the truth, France is not really into online shops. Most of the gold is to be found on the ground, so you may find yourself looking up some of these stores only to get the impression that I have gone mad. Please don't judge a Parisian by their website; they can't help it if they have better things to do than build you an online shop. Either they don't have them, or they are terrible, or they tend not to ship overseas. But don't give up that easily, there is always a way...

1. Find a French friend. Not only do you have someone to coucher avec next time you visit, but you can use their address for all your online purchases. Then you just have to convince them to post it on.

2. Use a forwarding service. Surprisingly, there are not that many options when it comes to sending on mail from Paris. Sure, ex-UK or US no problem, but no one seems to have cottoned on to this industry in Paris. Maybe they think they have to hand-deliver it or something?

3. Get your little bit of Paris via one of the many online boutiques exploiting France's lack of interest in the digital age. Net-a-porter and Farfetch have a good selection of French designers, including the biggies (Carven, Chloé) and independents like Sessun and Shine. ASOS also has a pretty good selection of the smaller labels and ships everywhere really fast (and generally free). *Bon magasinage*!

Le Getting Around

Taxis in Paris are easy but not as cheap as in New York nor as speedy as the Metro. It can also be slightly problematic if you have no French and the driver has no English. It can make for a long trip. Not that that's always a bad thing – I've made a few friends of cab drivers in Paris over a joint frustration and love of singing along to the radio.

BICYCLE

The city has the world's biggest bike sharing network, Vélib', which is run by the Paris town hall. Simply pick up a bike at a bike station (and they are everywhere, seriously, every 300 metres), then when you get too drunk or have too much shopping or become too lazy, you can dump it at the next bike station. And no helmet rules mean no helmet hair. Buy yourself a 1-day or a 7-day bike subscription (at the bike station) and away you go. Happy note: Riding a bike around Paris will be one of the highlights of your trip. I promise.

Get over your fear of getting lost underground and get on the Metro. You'll feel so proud of yourself for being so up with the locals that you'll forget you have absolutely no idea where you are. And trust me, once you do, it'll be your best friend (if you can get past the smell of urine, the petty thieves and the entire-family-busking productions, that is). When you have the hang of the map and the coloured lines (and working out you are heading in the right direction), you will find the Metro to be almost magical. It is such a great way to see Paris. It's like a travelator – trains are fast, they connect well, arriving every few minutes – it's a breeze. And there is something really nice about not knowing what to expect when your head pops up out of the station. Some places grungy, some like castles. Some places cool, some with gangsters. It's like location lucky dip! Except with those wee smells.

Never tried it. The system boggles me still, what with all the one-way streets and traffic and criss-cross lines. Even the website does my head in. But best of luck should you deem it a challenge you wish to take.

Paris isn't actually that big (geographically speaking) so walking is really one of the best ways to see the city. Plus it's the perfect antidote for all the croissants you'll be eating. Slightly gross note: Paris was once renowned for having more dog poo per footstep than any other city in the world. Fortunately they've cleaned up their act, so you can't really put a foot wrong these days.

Department Stores

Parisians love their department stores. And it's no wonder why – they are truly beautiful and have everything you need under one (amazingly designed) roof. While I always prefer the little man over the fat cat, these stores are an exception. And if you're into VAT refunds this is the ticket (*see page 22 for more on VAT*). I sometimes think if I were the last person left on earth I'd make my home Le Bon Marché. Sure I'd get lonely but imagine my massive wardrobe.

GALERIES LAFAYETTE
Department Store

40 boulevard Haussmann
75009 Paris
Tel: *+33 1 42 82 34 56*
Open: *Monday–Saturday*
9.30am–8pm, until 9pm
on Thursday
Closed: *Sunday*
Metro: *Chaussée d'Antin –*
La Fayette
www.galerieslafayette.com

Galeries Lafayette is the Parisians'
go-to family department store. But for
us non-Parisians, there are plenty of
helpful English-speaking staff and
again that equally helpful tourist
tax refund. It's the department store
equivalent of spaghetti bolognese.
No one could complain that it was
unsatisfying, and you pretty much
always feel like it. Whether you find
something to buy is kind of irrelevant
ultimately, as the architecture is so
famous and so incredible that just
seeing it is enough. Maybe pasta
wasn't the right analogy after all?

LE BON MARCHÉ
Department Store

24 rue de Sèvres
75007 Paris
Tel: *+33 1 44 39 80 00*
Open: *Monday, Tuesday,*
Wednesday & Saturday
10am–8pm, Thursday
& Friday 10am–9pm
Closed: *Sunday*
Metro: *Sèvres – Babylone*
www.lebonmarche.com

Gustave Eiffel's mum must be so
proud. Not only did he design that
big tower but he is also responsible
for the most luxurious department
store in the world. With regular
in-store exhibitions, a magical
never-ending beauty hall, designers
including Stella McCartney, Chloé,
Comme des Garçons and an entire
space dedicated to Tsumori Chisato,
I know which Paris landmark I'd
prefer to visit. Just imagine if he had
built the tower on top of the store?
Actually, his mum might say that was
showing off.

URE

ARTS DÉCORATIFS BEAUX A   ÉCRITS SUR L ART   MONOGRAPHIES

< Previous page, and above: Le Bon Marché

DEPARTMENT STORES

PRINTEMPS
Department Store

64 boulevard Haussmann
75009 Paris
Tel: +33 1 42 82 57 87
Open: Monday–Saturday
9.35am–8pm, until 10pm
on Thursday
Closed: Sunday
Metro: Havre – Caumartin
www.printemps.com

Printemps covers everything you want from a Parisian department store – incredibly beautiful architecture, all the major fashion names you could hope for, good restaurants, beauty, personal shoppers (as if you need help!!) – all under that stunning, iconic art deco glass dome. And then there is the view – walking onto the terrace is like lifting the cloche on a juicy meal – from the Eiffel Tower to Montmartre, it's all you can eat (but with your eyes).

< Previous page: Printemps

Tuileries Gardens

AND SURROUNDS

If this book was a man's guide to getting women to fall in love with him, this chapter has all the answers. Lingerie shops, perfumeries, chocolatiers, macarons, posh hotels and the disgustingly romantic Tuileries Gardens are all within a lovers' stroll of one another. All the clichés of Paris are alive and well. You'd really have to be dead inside if you didn't feel something fluttering in your chest around here. If that's the case then I recommend starting your day with an espresso and an apple tart at Maxim's before hot soft-footing across to Repetto for some colour therapy. If you're still not feeling it make a stop at Fifi Chachnil and buy some expensive knickers before taking a breather at Colette for lunch and shopping with the cool kids. With any luck you should now be heading to Hôtel Costes for champagne in the fancy surrounds, where your saucy knickers may come in handy.

M OPÉRA

BOULEVARD DE LA MADELEINE

repetto

RUE DE LA PAIX

el costes

RUE SAINT-HONORÉ

colette

M TUILERIES

ANNICK GOUTAL
Last minute gold

14 rue de Castiglione
75001 Paris
Tel: *+33 1 42 60 52 82*
Open: *Daily 10am–7pm*
Metro: *Tuileries*
www.annickgoutal.com

I wish I was Annick Goutal. She was a pianist, turned model, turned perfumer. Her life was like a Hallmark movie where Audrey Tautou (or Kate Hudson in the inevitable US remake) plays the part of the charmed beauty whose path leads to international success – stores all over the place, her name in mosaics in rue Saint-Honoré, a family-run business, killer looks and 80s thick hair – all while smelling really, really good. Very cool fragrance shops, with amazing personal service in the way that only family-owned businesses know how.

BENJAMIN
The Help

9 place de la Madeleine
Galerie de la Madeleine 75008 Paris
Tel: *+33 1 40 17 00 51*
Open: *Tuesday–Saturday*
10.30/10.45am (approx.)–1.30pm,
then again from 2.30pm–4.30pm
(approximately!)
Closed: *Sunday & Monday*
Metro: *Madeleine*

The term 'old school' could not find a better home than Benjamin. Bespoke tailoring, alterations, whatever you want – just as long as you realise that 'opening hours are approximate and no one can be held to them'. Benjamin will open *sometime* after morning tea and close for lunch then will open again *sometime* after lunch until, well, whenever home time is declared. If you're bored you could play opening hours roulette? Just turn up and see how it spins. Old-school gambling, French style.

CARITA
Pampered Paris

*11 rue du Faubourg
Saint-Honoré 75008 Paris*
Tel: *+33 1 44 94 11 11*
Open: *Monday–Saturday
10am–6.30pm*
Closed: *Sunday*
Metro: *Concorde, Madeleine*
www.maisondebeautecarita.fr

Pampering is not really one of
my things. I am not one of those
women who are into being fussed
over and I am especially bad at
small talk with strangers who
are cutting my toenails. I am into
fanciness, however, so Carita fills
my brief – fancy environment,
beautiful (and perfectly on-trend)
Essie nail polish and a technician
who has absolutely no English. That,
my friend, is the trifecta. Add in a
perfect manicure and you're getting
closer to Parisian women's grooming
standards.

CHANTAL THOMASS
French knickers

*211 rue Saint-Honoré
75001 Paris*
Tel: *+33 1 42 60 40 56*
Open: *Monday–Saturday
11am–7pm*
Closed: *Sunday*
Metro: *Tuileries*
www.chantalthomass.fr

Chantal Thomass is a luxury lingerie
brand inspired by the French
themes of eroticism and seduction.
The impressive store is located on
rue Saint-Honoré and with pink
button-back walls, the space has a
truly French boudoir feel. Last year
Chantal Thomass launched her book,
L'Histoire de la Lingerie, exploring
the relationship between women and
their bodies, seduction and eroticism.
Later this year I will release my book
exploring the relationship between
women, chocolate, obsession and
regret. This is all because I saw
myself in one of Chantal's mirrors
with a g-string disappearing between
my cheeks.

Chantal Thomass

COLETTE
Très French

213 rue Saint-Honoré 75001 Paris
Tel: *+33 1 55 35 33 90*
Open: *Monday–Saturday*
11am–7pm
Closed: *Sunday*
Metro: *Tuileries,*
Palais Royal – Musée du Louvre
www.colette.fr

If you don't know Colette there are only two things I can think of. You don't have the internet, or you are a blind boy living on a farm. Or maybe you are a blind boy, on a farm, who doesn't have the internet. Colette is probably Paris's most famous contemporary shop, so if you haven't heard of it, bone up now, my little fashion traveller. Across three levels, Colette offers more than something for everyone. Women's and men's fashion (Comme des Garçons, Pucci, Carven, Rochas, Stella McCartney, We Are Handsome, Erdem, to name but a few), a cosmetics bar stocking all the very best from the affordable Topshop range to the not-so-affordable Joëlle Ciocco, music, Colette compilation CDs, art books, magazines, t-shirts – I find purchasing one thing from each category to be a very satisfying experience if you are into turning shopping into a game. (I am). Downstairs is a restaurant where the coffee is better than most in Paris. You can get a nice salad, but if you're anything like me you'll be trying to trick the hip hop dude next to you into swapping it for his pasta mountain. Shopping this hard requires carb loading.

FIFI CHACHNIL
French knickers

231 rue Saint-Honoré
75001 Paris
Tel: *+33 1 42 61 21 83*
Open: *Monday–Saturday*
11am–7pm
Closed: *Sunday*
Metro: *Tuileries*
www.fifichachnil.com

Sexy lingerie brand sold in a boudoir setting? I acknowledge these are not words that would usually come with a recommendation from me unless in sarcasm or in one of my many failed attempts to write a multi-million-copy-selling Mills & Boon novel. But, here I am recommending this shop for sexy lingerie sold in a boudoir setting. How about that?! Not just for the super-skinny, Fifi caters for those of us with real bums. They may be expensive but the return on investment is definitely worth it.

GOYARD
Last minute gold

233 rue Saint-Honoré
75001 Paris
Tel: *+33 1 42 60 57 04*
Open: *Monday–Saturday*
11am–7pm
Closed: *Sunday*
Metro: *Tuileries,*
Palais Royal – Musée du Louvre
www.goyard.com

The smell of leather and polish join together in an overwhelming rush when you walk into Goyard, luggage makers since 1853. (I'm told it's the smell of wealth.) My first instinct is to leave, thinking, 'I am an impostor. I must flee before anyone realises I don't belong.' But I can't – I am mesmerised by the signature chevron monogram on everything, the array of coloured leather and the shiny buckles. All I can think is how good it must be to travel with luggage as stunning as this. The small, fancy dog I happen to have in my handbag is also in awe – for she has spotted herself a new travel doggie bowl. 'Please, Mama, can I have it? It's only $1200. Aren't I worth it?' This promptly snaps me out of my stupor and brings me haltingly back to my reality – a reality where a $1200 doggie bowl is actually quite repulsive, no matter how beautiful. But oh, how it is beautiful.

LE LOVERS' DAY

Feel the love. Feel up your partner. Swoon your way through the city of romance. Just like two buttery croissants coming together to make a love heart, today is all about walking hand in hand, saucy knickers, afternoon champagne and unlocking your heart (or padlocking yourself to a bridge, depending on your definition of romance).

10.00AM
Ride a bike

While I wouldn't recommend holding hands while riding a bike, there's nothing sexier than feeling free and happy pedalling along the Seine. Whether it's the wind in your hair or watching your partner's ass on the bike in front, there's a two-wheeled reason why the French are the most romantic people in the world.

See page 25

11.00AM
Le Pont des Arts

Ride to this beautiful pedestrian bridge over the Seine and attach an engraved padlock to the railing. Throw the key into the river as a gesture of your love. Normally this kind of tourist-slash-sickly thing would make me queasy, but in the case of this bridge it just makes me want to set up a love lock stand – this joint is crawling with lovers dying to immortalise their love.

Quai du Louvre, Place de l'Institut, 75006 Paris

1.00PM
Tuileries Gardens

I believe this may be the most romantic place on earth. There are couples everywhere, the light is beautiful, it's a huge peaceful romance-expanse. Even the pigeons here can't keep their hands off each other (claws, wings, whatever). Walk from one end to the other and if you weren't in love at the start you will be trying to get a leg over by the end.

See page 36
Metro: Tuileries

4.00PM
Hôtel Costes

By now you will be the couple to whom others say, 'Get a room!' So, this is when you find a double couch in the dim bar at Hôtel Costes. Sink down in the cushions, no one will see you playing footsies, but if they do they will applaud you, for this is Paris. Drink champagne. If you're hungry, there's nothing sexier than the mashed potato here. Now get a room.

See page 57

3.00PM
Chantal Thomass

It only makes sense at this stage of the day to stop by luxury French lingerie store Chantal Thomass for something a little saucy. It's all about seduction (not that he'll need any convincing). Lace, silk, bows, frills, crutch or none ... Your choice depends on how far you want to take this day I suppose.

See page 42

LE LOVERS' TIP:

THE ONLY **THING** THE FRENCH LOVE
MORE THAN LOVE **IS EXPRESSING**
THEIR LOVE. IF YOU WANT **TO LOVE**
LIKE A LOCAL YOU NEED TO SPEAK
LIKE A LOCAL. IF YOU DON'T
KNOW ANY FRENCH **JUST MEMORISE**
THE LYRICS TO 'VOULEZ VOUS
COUCHER AVEC MOI **CE SOIR'.**
WHEN I WAS **LITTLE** I THOUGHT
IT WAS A SONG ABOUT ICE CREAM.
I GUESS I **WAS CLOSE WITH**
THE LICKING BIT.

HÔTEL COSTES

Très French

239 rue Saint-Honoré
75001 Paris
Tel: +33 1 42 44 50 00
Metro: Tuileries
www.hotelcostes.com

'*Where should I go in Paris, Michi?*'
Hôtel Costes. Sit in a velvet armchair,
eat cheese and drink champagne
served by teenage-looking models,
watch the people check in and out
for fashion week, and drink
some more while listening to the
soundtrack of fashion and money.

'*But I meant to shop.*' Why shop when
you can sit here and drink? I mean
it. No amount of French lingerie will
make you feel cooler or sexier than
sitting here and drinking. Promise.

JEAN PAUL HÉVIN CHOCOLATIER

Last minute gold

231 rue Saint-Honoré
75001 Paris
Tel: +33 1 55 35 35 96
Open: Monday–Saturday
10am–7.30pm
Closed: Sunday
Metro: Concorde, Tuileries, Opéra
www.jphevin.com

Amazing artisan chocolatiers are a
dime a dozen these days, chocolate
being so hot right now. But how often
do you see a stiletto in chocolate?
Only in fashion week perhaps, but
Jean Paul Hévin chocolates taste
good all year round (and they wrap
them nice and snug for the plane ride
home so they make the perfect gift).

LADURÉE
Très French

16 rue Royale 75008 Paris
Tel: *+33 1 42 60 21 79*
Open: *Monday–Thursday*
8am–7.30pm; Friday–Saturday
8am–8pm; Sundays & public
holidays 10am–7pm
Metro: *Concorde, Madeleine*
www.laduree.fr

From the outside of Ladurée you
would think David Beckham was
getting undressed in the window.
There is a sea of girls shoved up
against the glass taking endless
iPhone pictures and busily
Instagraming away. This macaron
shop is so famous that Hello Kitty
and Tsumori Chisato have both
contributed window designs.
I'd rather taste Becks' pecs, but
whatever floats your boat. If you're
a macaron fan, it doesn't get better
than this.

L'APPARTEMENT 217

Pampered Paris

217 rue Saint-Honoré
75001 Paris
Tel: *+33 1 42 96 00 96*
Open: *Tuesday–Saturday*
10am–7pm
Closed: *Sunday*
Metro: *Tuileries*
www.lappartement217.com

If you have ever seen the movie
L'Appartement, you will know that
it makes absolutely no sense. Boy
meets girl, leaves girl in Tokyo, goes
to Paris, meets another girl, starts
stalking her, hides in her apartment,
sleeps with a different girl thinking
it is THE girl … It's a nightmare
that no one can follow. Anyway, this
place is nothing like that except the
name. It's a fancy spa specialising in
skincare and massage.

MAXIM'S

Sit and sip

3 rue Royale 75008 Paris
Tel: *+33 1 42 65 27 94*
Open: *Lunch: 12.30pm–2pm,*
Dinner: 7.30pm–10pm
Closed: *Sunday & Monday*
during July & August
Metro: *Concorde*
www.maxims-de-paris.com

It's 1900. You are dating an artist
in Paris, life is sweet. It's full of
optimism and hope. The arts are
blooming, your beau is hot and in-
demand. Every afternoon you two slip
out of your love nest for coffee and
chocolate at Maxim's. The waiter is
cheeky and flirtatious. Get the idea?
Well absolutely nothing has changed
at Maxim's, except you possibly get
up earlier and your artist BF is poor.
Maxim's won't let you down like he
might – it's sweet and opulent and a
perfect pit stop on the way down to
the Tuileries Gardens.

PETIT BATEAU

Très French

9 rue du 29 Juillet
75001 Paris
Tel: +33 1 42 96 28 15
Open: Monday–Saturday
10am–7pm
Closed: Sunday
Metro: Tuileries
www.petit-bateau.com

Petit Bateau is the home of French cotton basics and nicely nautical stripes. It is an institution, a house of cotton basics like no other. In 1918, Étienne Valton cut some length off his boxer shorts and invented underpants. Wasn't that a great idea? I have no idea what anyone wore before this, but we can all breathe a sigh of relief that the man who founded Petit Bateau had this brainwave. After refining them a touch, the basic Petit Bateau knickers were made – and we are all still wearing them to this day. Sure, we have to squeeze into the kids' ones (they are way cooler than the adults' ones, trust me), but that's not a bad thing – forever sixteen, in my pants at least.

REPETTO

Shoes, bags, dog collars

22 rue de la Paix
75002 Paris
Tel: +33 1 44 71 83 12
Open: Monday–Saturday
9.30am–7.30pm
Closed: Sunday
Metro: Opéra
www.repetto.com

Rose Repetto began creating ballet shoes in 1947 and has since expanded to offer the most incredibly vast array of dancewear and snazzy shoes. Last time I went to Paris I had a request for 'light red, patent leather ballet flats'. Even as I was promising to look, it never occurred to me that I would actually find any. I was already thinking about which snow dome I'd bring home with me. Lo and behold, Repetto and the giant rainbow of shoes had just that. They were at least one hundred times more expensive than the snow dome but still, I felt like Santa handing them over. Repetto has also collaborated with the likes of Yohji Yamamoto and Comme des Garçons, making it not only satisfying giving but also very cool.

The Palais Royal

AND SURROUNDS

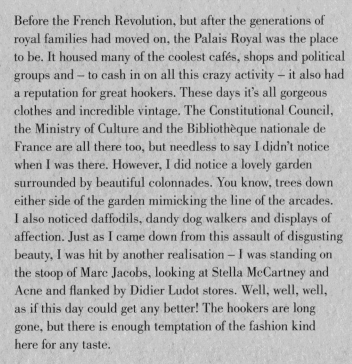

Before the French Revolution, but after the generations of royal families had moved on, the Palais Royal was the place to be. It housed many of the coolest cafés, shops and political groups and – to cash in on all this crazy activity – it also had a reputation for great hookers. These days it's all gorgeous clothes and incredible vintage. The Constitutional Council, the Ministry of Culture and the Bibliothèque nationale de France are all there too, but needless to say I didn't notice when I was there. However, I did notice a lovely garden surrounded by beautiful colonnades. You know, trees down either side of the garden mimicking the line of the arcades. I also noticed daffodils, dandy dog walkers and displays of affection. Just as I came down from this assault of disgusting beauty, I was hit by another realisation – I was standing on the stoop of Marc Jacobs, looking at Stella McCartney and Acne and flanked by Didier Ludot stores. Well, well, well, as if this day could get any better! The hookers are long gone, but there is enough temptation of the fashion kind here for any taste.

RUE DE
Kitsuné
AVENUE DE L'OPÉRA
RUE DE RICHELIEU
Didier Ludot
RUE DE MONTPENSIER
RUE SA
M PALAIS ROYAL
MUSÉE DU LO

TS CHAMPS

Maison Fabre

Acne

RUE CROIX DES PETIT CHAMPS

UE DE VALOIS

ONORÉ

Musée du Louvre

Acne

ACNE
The cool gang

124 Galerie de Valois
75001 Paris
Tel: +33 1 42 60 16 62
Open: Monday–Saturday
11am–7pm
Closed: Sunday
Metro: Palais Royal –
Musée du Louvre
www.acnestudios.com

If I told you that I looked for the
Acne store in Le Marais for days
without success, would you think less
of me? I don't know what happened,
but I later found out it was a few
doors from my apartment. Like dust,
I guess – you miss it if you're too
close. But I didn't miss this one. It
was full of Americanos rubbing up
with the gorgeous Swedish staff. It is
like all the Acne stores – impossible
to pick fault with and always a
pleasant experience, with really
good-looking staff. The product isn't
bad either – denim, knits, great
coats, unisex and very fashion. Oh
and they really know how to retail,
those Scandos.

DIDIER LUDOT
Paris vintage

20 Galerie de Montpensier
Jardin du Palais Royal
75001 Paris
Tel: +33 1 42 96 06 56
Open: Monday–Saturday
10.30am–7pm
Metro: Palais Royal –
Musée du Louvre
www.didierludot.fr

You get the feeling when walking
down the colonnade and coming
to Didier Ludot's fifth shopfront,
that this guy owns the joint. He is
a legend in vintage haute couture
(to name a niche), and has been in
this space since 1975. This place
is something to behold. On any
given day you may find a 1967 Dior
feathered pantsuit, a 1982 Lacroix
beaded top, 1957 Ferragamo ballet
flats, 1934 Hermès mirror, Mugler
cuff – need I continue? I swear I'm
not making it up, this place is gold.
Be sure to cross over to the La Petite
Robe Noire sister boutique on the
opposite side of the Palais Royal.
Ludot's the (French, vintage, haute
couture) man.

GABRIELLE GEPPERT
Shoes, bags, dog collars/
Paris vintage

31–34 Galerie de Montpensier
Jardin du Palais Royal
75001 Paris
Tel: *+33 1 42 61 53 52*
Open: *Monday–Saturday*
10.30am–7pm
Closed: *Sunday*
Metro: *Palais Royal –*
Musée du Louvre
www.gabriellegeppert.com

Gabrielle Geppert is tiny and very cute. She has long, beautiful pale grey-lemon hair and a serious passion for accessories. So to hear that she was recently held up at gunpoint for her Hermès comes as quite a shock. She is so small and pretty and has such a lovely collection. 'Hermès is like gold in Paris,' she tells me. And coming to her vintage accessories store, I believe her. Hermès jewellery, Pucci sunnies, Louis Vuitton handbags ... it's a small white heaven. Just be sure to take heaps of money. You'll happily hand it over.

KITSUNÉ
The cool gang

52 rue de Richelieu 75002 Paris
Tel: +33 1 42 60 34 28
Open: Monday–Saturday
11am–7.30pm
Closed: Sunday
Metro: Pyramides,
Palais Royal – Musée du Louvre
www.kitsune.fr

Even the approach to Kitsuné is delicious. Just walking down rue de Richelieu is a delight. It feels like being on a film set – gorgeous Parisian street; two tiny shops straddling a walkway to the Jardin du Palais Royal; a view down past Verjus, a lovely bar/restaurant (get there after 6pm). The shop on the left is t-shirts only, the one on the right houses the label's main range. Kitsuné is a very cool French brand known for classic, contemporary staples – jersey dresses, sweatshirts, tees or classic cashmere knits. Spot-on detailing and beautiful quality are reflected in kind of weighty prices (over €100 for a t-shirt), but the hot shop boy will distract you from your wallet.

LES ARTS DÉCORATIFS
Très French

107 rue de Rivoli
75001 Paris
Tel: +33 1 44 55 57 50
Open: Tuesday–Sunday
11am–6pm, until 9pm on Thursday
Closed: Monday
Metro: Tuileries
www.lesartsdecoratifs.fr

I know I project an image of a well-
rounded culture vulture, but let's
face it, we are all in Paris for the
shops. Which is precisely why I
feel it necessary to let you know
that you can, without lie, tell your
Facey friends and your mum that you
really enjoyed Les Arts Décoratifs.
Shop, that is. Within this (actually
very interesting and lovely) museum
there is a very nice gift shop indeed.
No harm, no foul. Perfect for gifts
for the suckers left behind – books,
jewellery, ceramics, stationery.

MAISON FABRE
Très French

128–129 Galerie de Valois
75001 Paris
Tel: +33 1 42 60 75 88
Open: Monday–Saturday
11am–7pm
Closed: Sunday
Metro: Pyramides,
Palais Royal – Musée du Louvre
www.maisonfabre.com

I adore this shop. It is so single-
minded – they just make gloves.
The Fabre family has been designing
and manufacturing their own gloves
since 1924, against many odds (not
the least of which is that people
hardly wear gloves anymore . . .).
The lovely Olivier, the new
generation of Fabre, cuts a dashing
figure in the store. He's good for
business too, he's very handsome –
the man could sell gloves to a goat,
I reckon. Not that he needs to try,
these gloves sell themselves. Made
with hand stitches and family love.

Maison Fabre

MARC JACOBS
The cool gang

34 rue de Montpensier
75001 Paris
Tel: +33 1 55 35 02 60
Open: Monday–Saturday
11am–7pm
Closed: Sunday
Metro: Pyramides,
Palais Royal – Musée du Louvre
www.marcjacobs.com

Marc Jacobs' stores are like rabbits.
Or mutant rabbits actually – they
are everywhere but in various forms,
never quite offering the entire
rabbit, if you know what I mean.
This store is big and luxurious. No
crowds fighting over umbrellas like
in SoHo, just a calm and beautiful
environment and a lot of helpful
staff. This store has the whole Marc
Jacobs ready-to-wear collection,
accessories, menswear and some
kids' clothes. Oh, and a wall of bags.
No rabbit leather that I could see,
but I wouldn't be surprised.

GOOD TIMES LE DAY

Hedonism is an art. It takes dedication and commitment to act upon the belief that pleasure is the highest good. Follow these steps of a truly devoted decadent and, even if you are slightly out of your comfort zone eating liver and watching topless cabaret, I promise that by the end of today you'll know how to live for the good times.

1.00PM
Restaurant le Meurice

The hardcore hedonist finds lunch in the most opulent dining room on earth with foie gras and blue lobster the perfect start. It's really expensive and the need for booking months in advance takes some of the spontaneity out of the day, but even the devil makes plans.

228 rue de Rivoli,
75001 Paris
Book online at www.lemeurice.com/
le-meurice-restaurant

3.00PM
7L Librairie

I once got caught stalking Karl Lagerfeld in Colette, then ended up photographed for Vice magazine under the headline 'Girls who fucked up in Colette'. If that's not the devil's work I don't know what is. Karl is not always at his bookshop but some have reported sightings there among weighty art and fashion books.

7 rue de Lille,
75007 Paris
Open: *Tuesday–Saturday*
10am–7.30pm
Closed: *Sunday & Monday*
www.librairie7l.com

4.00PM
Sonia Rykiel

Enter the hermetically sealed silence of the Sonia Rykiel store and the world is left behind. Then walk around a mirrored corner and bonjour, bonjour! What have we here? A wall of sex toys. Funny, and awkward.

See page 188

5.00PM
Palais de Tokyo

To cleanse yourself of dildos, a bit of contemporary art is always good. Then you can repurpose your sexploits as 'postmodern' to justify them. Palais de Tokyo was reopened in April 2012 and houses some of the best contemporary art you'll ever see.

13 avenue du Président Wilson, 75116 Paris
***Metro:** Alma-Marceau, Iéna*
www.palaisdetokyo.com

8.00PM
Derrière

Dinner at Derrière is an absolute must when in Paris. At the back of a beautiful courtyard and made up of a series of living rooms, this old apartment is magical. You can play ping pong and you can smoke upstairs in the bedroom. Party time.

See page 17

10.30PM
The Crazy Horse

Daggy perhaps, but still, think of it as ironic. Ending the day with a bottle of champagne and the 10.45pm show at The Crazy Horse will make you laugh and keep the good times rolling in to the night.

12 avenue George V, 75008 Paris
***Show times:** Sunday–Friday 8.15pm & 10:45pm, Saturday 7.00 pm, 9.30pm & 11.45pm*
Book online at reservation@lecrazyhorseparis.com

LE GOOD TIMES TIP:

FOR SOME REASON PARIS NEVER GOT
THE MEMO THAT SMOKING KILLS.
EITHER THAT OR THEY JUST PREFER
A GOOD TIME TO A LONG TIME.
IF YOU WANT TO LOOK LIKE
YOU BELONG, COVER YOURSELF
IN NICOTINE PATCHES IN THE
MONTHS LEADING UP TO YOUR TRIP:
BY THE TIME YOU ARRIVE YOU'LL
BE READY TO COUGH UP A LUNG
LIKE A LOCAL.

PIERRE HARDY
Shoes, bags, dog collars

156 Galerie de Valois Jardin
du Palais Royal 75001 Paris
Tel: *+33 1 42 60 59 75*
Open: *Monday–Saturday*
11am–7pm
Closed: *Sunday*
Metro: *Palais Royal –*
Musée du Louvre
www.pierrehardy.com

At first glance Pierre Hardy looks
like a nightclub. A dark and drug-
filled nightclub – all black mirrored
walls and dark carpet. At second
glance, you can see this is a shop
that takes its shoes very seriously.
Rumour has it that Pierre Hardy
shoes elongate the leg. I find this
a little hard to swallow, but I believe
most rumours start with some kind
of fact, so I am willing to give him
the benefit of the doubt. After all,
we all know that there really are mole
people living in the Metro, right?
So leg-lengthening shoes shouldn't
be a stretch should it? Pardon le pun.

SHISEIDO BY SERGE LUTENS
Pampered Paris

142 Galerie de Valois
75001 Paris
Tel: +33 1 49 27 09 09
Open: Monday–Saturday
10am–7pm
Closed: Sunday
Metro: Palais Royal –
Musée du Louvre
www.sergelutens.com

Stepping into this shop is like
walking straight into a Tim Burton
film. Opulent, gothic, dark, dramatic.
The door is locked which is
confronting, but get over it and press
the buzzer – the ladies inside are not
a bit Burton-esque. They are lovely
and friendly and have perfumers
willing to help you create a bespoke
fragrance from the million options.
Or they can help you pick one of the
many mixed fragrances off the shelf,
finding the perfect whiff for you. It's
gorgeous and fun and very fancy.

STELLA MCCARTNEY PARIS
The cool gang

114-121 Galerie de Valois
75001 Paris
Tel: +33 1 47 03 03 80
Open: Monday–Saturday
10.30am–7pm
Closed: Sunday
Metro: Palais Royal –
Musée du Louvre
www.stellamccartney.com

You know how Stella McCartney
always looks so shiny and fresh?
Well so does her Paris shop. And
you know how she has that cheeky
sparkle in her eye? Well so do
the clothes. The shop is triple
fronted and sectioned into lingerie,
sunglasses, ready-to-wear and a
small kids corner. Cheeky prints,
really playful children's wear and
lingerie that hits that perfect point
between posh and pervy.

Hôtel de Ville

From 1310 until 1802, Place de l'Hôtel de Ville was called Place de Grève. In what I believe was a very wise decision, the government changed the name of the square outside Hôtel de Ville, the public administration buildings near the Seine, when they stopped killing people there. Prior to that, it was the place to be for executions. Beheaded, quartered, cooked up, guillotined or burned at the stake; you name it, they tried it. Things have changed these days, with ice skating taking the place of the bloodshed and a crêpe van replacing the formerly useful guillotine.

Located in the 4th arrondissement and a stone's throw from Notre Dame, popping up out of this Metro stop elicits the thought, 'Good grief, everything is so old!'. Walk north for a bit however, and you'll come to the Centre Pompidou at the opposite end of the architectural spectrum. Some great vintage (Free'P'Star), a few pampering delights (Sephora, Sultane de Saba) and some easy classics (H&M) are all to be had around here. And if it's all getting too nice for you, you can always watch the skaters for a while and hope to see a finger guillotined.

RUE MONTMARTRE

Kiliwatch

Mokuba

LES HALLES Ⓜ

RUE DU LOUVRE

RUE DE RIVOLI

Sephora

Ⓜ PONT NEUF

CHÂTELET Ⓜ

H

RUE ÉTIENNE MARCEL

Ⓜ ÉTIENNE
MARCEL

BOULEVARD DE SÉBASTOPOL

● Centre Pompidou

Free'P'star ●

ABOVE HÔTEL DE VILLE

BY TERRY
Pampered Paris

21 & 36 Galerie Véro-Dodat
75001 Paris
Tel: +33 1 44 76 00 76
Open: Monday–Saturday
10.30am–7pm
Closed: Sunday
Metro: Louvre – Rivoli
www.byterry.com

When you hear that Terry de Gunzburg is ex-YSL and read phrases describing her legendary makeup as 'Photoshop in a brush', it is hard to walk past this luxuriously elegant store. And having just been in Christian Louboutin around the corner with more remodelled faces than I care to recall, I really need a little bit of Terry's magic. Faultless foundation is just the beginning for this cosmetic heaven – go in and you come out with a whole new face.

EPISODE
Paris vintage

12–16 rue Tiquetonne
75002 Paris
Tel: +33 1 42 61 14 65
Open: Monday 1pm–8pm;
Tuesday–Friday 11.30am–9.30pm;
Saturday 11am–8pm
Closed: Sunday
Metro: Étienne Marcel
www.episode.eu

We have an Episode second-hand clothes shop in my neighbourhood at home, so to find another store in Paris makes me feel somewhat cheated. I like to suspend the disbelief that someone chose all my vintage pieces carefully, scoured old ladies' wardrobes or bought deceased estates and edited them to perfection. Alas, the business of vintage is alive and well in this giant Paris outpost of the Amsterdam-based vintage clothing chain. Still, if you like your vintage on a mega level, Episode has it covered.

ETAM
Cheap and cheerful

67–73 rue de Rivoli 75001 Paris
Tel: *+33 1 44 76 73 73*
Open: *Monday–Saturday*
10am–7.30pm
Closed: *Sunday*
Metro: *Châtelet*
www.etam.fr

This is the thing about Paris: everything is written in French, therefore everything looks fancy. So if you need to take home presents but you want to spend the big bucks on yourself, Etam is the place. This massive mid-market flagship has its own label alongside a wealth of other (almost fashionable) affordable brands – and seeing as they all have French names and care labels, the undies you buy for your sister could have come from anywhere.

FREE'P'STAR
Paris vintage

61 rue de la Verrerie 75004 Paris
Tel: *+33 1 42 78 00 76*
Open: *Monday–Saturday*
11am–9pm, Sunday 2pm–9pm
Metro: *Hôtel de Ville*
www.freepstar.com

Any Parisian worth her Hermès knows Free'P'Star. The name of this two-boutique chain is a play on the French word *friperie*, which means thrift shop. It could also be roughly translated as 'a giant mess of a shop with vintage gold hidden everywhere'. Burberry trench anyone? Hermès scarf perhaps? What about a fur – there are plenty! There is a small room upstairs which is lit with blue neon – great for finding that elusive 70s disco number, not so good for finding a vein.

ABOVE HÔTEL DE VILLE

LE FREE DAY

We all want to stay in Paris for as long as we possibly can, so every now and then, a non-consumer day is required. That may not sound terribly fun, but hear me out: the more you can save on food and travel, the more you can spend on clothes. Surely that's worth being tight for?

9.00AM
Walk the Canal Saint-Martin

After eating as much as possible at home, get yourself to the Canal Saint-Martin (Metro to Gare du Nord if you have a ticket in your pocket). Skip some stones at the lock, a la Amélie. Enjoy the sunshine. Spot some Space Invader mosaics in the nearby streets. Exercise and art . . . check!

See pages 110–113

10.00AM
Artazart

I love design books – to tell if they are any good try to judge them by their cover. If you are right, then it's good design. Drop in to this beautiful bookstore and disappear for a while among mountains of books on graphic design, interior design, architecture and art.

83 quai de Valmy, 75010 Paris
Tel: +33 1 40 40 24 00
Open: Daily
www.artazart.com

12.00PM
Louvre

If it's the first Sunday of the month, Bastille Day, or a Friday between 6pm and 9pm and you happen to be under 26, then you can get into the Louvre for free. Or if you're under 18 and a member of the EU, or an artist affiliated to the Maison des Artistes. Sorry, but could you be a little more specific?

www.louvre.fr

1.30PM
Marché Raspail

By now you'll be totally starving. As we are on a spending-ban, it's off to market we go. Marché Raspail would have to be one of the most expensive food markets known to man, but that's ok, we ain't buying, we're just snacking. 'Could I please taste the brie? Oh those strawberries look a little too ripe, may I taste?' Repeat until full.

Boulevard Raspail
75006 Paris
Tuesday & Friday 7.00am–2.30pm,
Sunday 7.00am–3.00pm
Metro: Rennes, Sèvre-Babylone

3.00PM
Galeries Lafayette

Don't let anyone say I don't give you the hot tips. This one is a scorcher. Every Friday at 3pm Galeries Lafayette holds fashion shows in the store. The show is free but you will need to book at welcome@galerieslafayette.com. Pretend you're an Olsen and sit in the front row.

See page 30

6.00PM
Paris Plage

If it's July or August, spend twilight playing on the pretend summer beach on the banks of the Seine. Hilariously cute. Pétanque and volleyball are free. Surreal, but true.

Pompidou Expressway,
right bank of the Seine

LE FREE DAY TIP

PARIS HAS A DODGY SIDE. THAT'S WHY I LOVE HER. ONE MINUTE SHE'S ALL CHRISTIAN LACROIX, THE NEXT SHE'S TRYING TO FLEECE YOU FOR DONATIONS WHILE POSING AS A DEAF MUTE WEARING AN IPOD. BUT THERE IS MUCH TO LEARN (AHEM, EARN) FROM THESE SCAMSTERS. IF YOU'RE LOOKING TO EARN A BIT ON THE SIDE LEARN A SKILL BEFORE YOU LEAVE. FOR WHAT IT'S WORTH, I FIND MIMING EASY AND VAGUELY FASHIONABLE AS YOU CAN WEAR STRIPES.

H&M
Cheap and cheerful

120 rue de Rivoli
75001 Paris
Tel: *+33 1 55 34 96 86*
Open: *Monday–Saturday*
10am–8pm
Closed: *Sunday*
Metro: *Châtelet*
www.hm.com

H&M. Helpful & Mandatory. Healing & Meaningful. Handy & Magnificent. Heavenly & Made-for-you. Am I making my point? This Swedish chain-store giant can solve *any* outfit emergency you may have. Given that H&M recently solved my emergency involving the overwhelming desire for a gold fisherman-style sweater, I don't think this is an overstatement. You want something specific? Just go to H&M.

KILIWATCH
Paris vintage

64 rue Tiquetonne
75002 Paris
Tel: *+33 1 42 21 17 37*
Open: *Monday 2pm–7.15pm;*
Tuesday–Saturday 11am–7.45pm
Closed: *Sunday*
Metro: *Étienne Marcel*
www.espacekiliwatch.fr

There was an announcement on the Parisian P.A. system that went something like, 'Quick!!! The world is about to explode and the only way you can be spared is to buy heaps of vintage stuff at Kiliwatch!!!' And, gee, are those skinny hipsters obedient – the place is heaving with them. They're rifling through walls of denim, arty books, old fashion magazines and racks of vintage finds helpfully curated into sections based on a look (hippy, rocker, geek chic). If you do happen to survive after the explosion, be sure to dress well – there is not a nerd in sight in this hipster heaven.

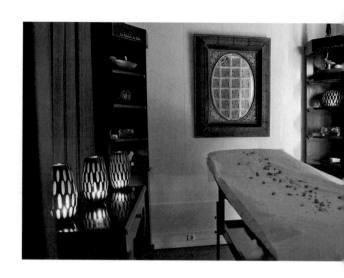

LA DROGUERIE
The Help

9–11 rue du Jour
75001 Paris
Tel: *+33 1 45 08 93 27*
Open: *Monday 2pm–6.45pm,*
Tuesday–Saturday
10.30am–6.45pm
Closed: *Sunday*
Metro: *Les Halles,*
Étienne Marcel
www.ladroguerie.com

Beautiful haberdashery with one of
the biggest, and finest, selections of
trims, buttons and ribbons. Knitting
patterns for those of you who knit,
sewing bits for the sewers. Not much
for me but a pain in my brain at my
extreme lack of skills.

LA SULTANE DE SABA
Pampered Paris

8 bis rue Bachaumont
75002 Paris
Tel: *+33 1 40 41 90 95*
Open: *Monday–Friday*
10.30am–7.30pm,
until 10pm on Thursday
Closed: *Sunday*
Metro: *Étienne Marcel*
www.lasultanedesaba.com

This is the kind of place Major
Healey spent all those years trying
to get into behind Major Nelson's
back. The treasured confines of *I
Dream of Jeannie*'s bottle is exactly
what it's like at La Sultane de Saba –
chandeliers, velvet plush cushions,
dim lighting and a whole lot of people
pandering to your every whim. Chuck
in the half-hour 'Cinnamon slimming
massage' and all your wishes are
granted. Heaven on earth.

La Sultane de Saba

ABOVE HÔTEL DE VILLE

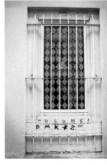

MOKUBA
The Help

18 rue Montmartre
75001 Paris
Tel: +33 1 40 13 81 41
Open: Monday–Friday
9.30am–6.30pm
Closed: Saturday & Sunday
Metro: Étienne Marcel,
Les Halles
www.mokuba.fr

There is a huge resurgence in all
things craft at the moment. The last
decade has seen more and more
mothers take up knitting, fathers take
up sewing, and every second schmo
take up blogging and baking. To all
of you who have entered this world of
putting birds and owls on everything,
this is the shop for you. Buttons,
trims, ribbons, Liberty fabric – it's
Club X for crafters. And little girls.
And me. Who doesn't love a ribbon?

NAF NAF
Cheap and cheerful

33 rue Étienne Marcel
75001 Paris
Tel: +33 1 42 33 31 41
Open: Monday–Saturday
10am–7pm
Closed: Sunday
Metro: Étienne Marcel
www.nafnaf.com

When I was a little girl my dad
bought me a Naf Naf tracksuit in
Paris. At the time (bearing in mind
I was twelve), I thought it was the
coolest thing ever. The brand found
success in 1983 with its cult cotton
all-in-one combination and has since
diversified into accessories, glasses,
swimwear and lingerie. Somehow Naf
Naf has grown to become an iconic
mass-market brand and is a firm
fixture on high streets across France.
I think it is a little naf naf but all
those Parisians can't be wrong can
they? You'll have to make up your
own mind. Look here for basics with
a nod to fashion, staples and cheap
accessories.

PROMOD
Cheap and cheerful

110 rue de Rivoli
75001 Paris
Tel: +33 1 40 39 09 24
Open: Monday–Saturday
9.30am–8pm
Closed: Sunday
Metro: Châtelet
www.promod.fr

On first glance you may be excused for thinking that you are stuck in a 1987 cheap chain store. The music is terrible, none of the fabric can go near naked flames and the racks are packed closer than a hamburger, but the good news is that the prices are also from a long-gone decade. If you can stand it, sifting through the dross can pay off. A cardi of mine from here has actually been mistaken for Marni and it cost the same amount as a hamburger.

Room Service

ROOM SERVICE
Paris vintage

52 rue d'Argout
75002 Paris
Tel: +33 1 77 11 27 24
Open: Monday–Saturday
11am–7.30pm
Closed: Sunday
Metro: Sentier, Étienne Marcel
www.roomservice.fr

I wouldn't classify Room Service
as vintage, more odds and sods.
There is some last-season clothing
(some new with tags), some vintage,
some current season and then some
samples. The last time I was there
I bought a necklace made in the
store by the shop assistant. The table
running through the store is covered
in her jewellery-making kit, and
buying from the maker is a really
nice experience. Well, at least it was
until she vanished down a trap door
in the floor for half an hour, leaving
me to man the desk. Weird of her,
but the necklace is still a fave.

SEPHORA
Pampered Paris

75 rue de Rivoli
75001 Paris
Tel: +33 1 40 13 16 50
Open: Monday–Saturday
10am–8pm, until 9pm
on Thursday
Closed: Sunday
Metro: Louvre – Rivoli
www.sephora.fr

If you haven't heard of Sephora, you
are either a hermit or a man. There
are a few Sephoras in Paris, every
one as jaw-droppingly magnificent
as the last. With wall-to-wall beauty
products, each branch carries a good
cross-section of mid-to-high end
beauty, fragrance, skin and haircare
brands, including the full Sephora
range. It's impossible to explore it
all, so my advice is to duck under a
counter at closing time and have a
lock-in. Trust me, no one will notice,
the place is massive.

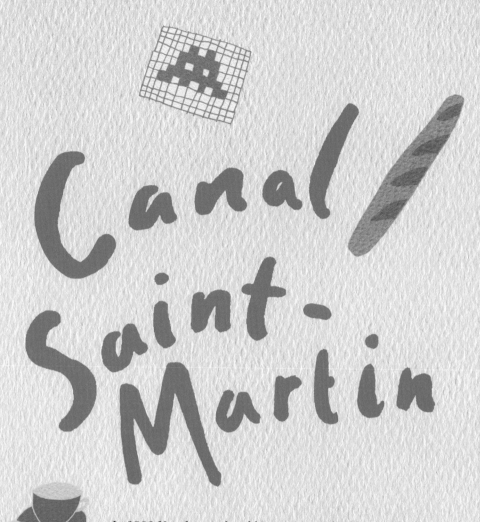

Canal Saint-Martin

In 1802 Napoleon ordered his minions to build a canal to supply fresh water to the city. The water might not be too fresh today but the area around Canal Saint-Martin is full of fresh talent – emerging shops and amazing street art. Devoid of touristy landmarks and full of generosity, Canal Saint-Martin is local Paris at its best. Start your day with a coffee and baguette at Chez Prune (god knows you won't get an egg), and then get lost in the maze of streets that flank the canal. It's sort of like a mini Amsterdam, relaxed (but not as stoned) and with much cooler shops. Agnès B, A.P.C., and Veja Centre Commercial are highlights but there are little surprises around every corner. If you're into street art keep your eyes peeled for Space Invader mosaics. It's like the mother ship around here. I don't think Napoleon would approve – he was more a small man than a Pac-Man kinda guy.

BOULEVARD DE MAGENTA

RUE DU CHÂTEAU D'EAU

RUE DE LANCRY

Agnès B

RUE

Veja Centre
Commercial

METROPOLITAIN

M
RÉPUBLIQUE

Pink Flamingo

RSEILLE

Chez Prune

QUAI DE JEMMAPES

QUAI DE VALMY

E YVES TOUDIC

AGNÈS B
Affordable chic

13 rue de Marseille
75010 Paris
Tel: +33 1 42 06 66 58
Open: Winter: Monday–Saturday
10am–7pm. Summer: Monday–
Saturday 10.30am–7.30pm
Closed: Sunday
Metro: Jacques Bonsergent,
République
www.agnesb.com

I got into trouble from the lady in
Agnès B. I was so enamoured by
this store that I was caught taking
photos. Obviously you won't see
many here as she destroyed the film
(theoretically, as I actually have
an iPhone not a 35mm). She was
so French too – calm, strict, stern,
restrained, considered. Oh, hang on,
maybe she was Agnès B? Clothes
that epitomise France in their good
taste and restraint – you can't go
wrong here. Children's clothes are
reasonably priced, very cool and
beautifully made.

A.P.C.
The cool gang

5 rue de Marseille
75010 Paris
Tel: +33 1 42 39 84 46
Open: Monday–Saturday
11.30am–8pm, Sunday
1.30pm–7.30pm
Metro: Jacques Bonsergent,
République
www.apc.fr

Did you know that sometimes I see
people and numbers as colours?
I don't have synesthesia officially,
but I do have this strange association
thing going on. Anyway, before you
think I am nuts, hear me out. It just
might make sense to you when you
walk into this store. Deep navy is
my favourite colour ever. It's broody
and beautiful, simple and classic.
It suits everyone and always looks
good and is reserved for my best
friends or people I admire. There
are not that many of them, but they
are an extraordinary bunch. A.P.C.
is navy blue. Very French, classic,
timeless and terribly fashionable.
You can't go past A.P.C. for denim
and outerwear especially.

VEJA CENTRE COMMERCIAL
Look at me!

2 rue de Marseille 75010 Paris
Tel: *+33 1 42 02 26 08*
Open: *Monday 1pm–7.30pm,*
Tuesday–Saturday 11am–8pm
Closed: *Sunday*
Metro: *Jacques Bonsergent,*
République
www.centrecommercial.cc

Two steps from the Canal Saint-
Martin, the founders of Veja – the
French eco-friendly trainers and
accessories label – came up with the
idea of mixing their own products
in with a selection of other fashion
brands including Saint James,
Camilla Norrback, Nu, Repetto and
Grenson to create a new concept
retail space. Alongside clothes and
accessories, you can find original
1950s furniture, vintage bikes, bio
cosmetics and a selection of books.
The space is airy and beautifully
edited and arranged. I wonder if my
book will make it in there? If it does,
I'd like it to be on that nice sunny
spot on the centre table as you walk
in, please. Like a cat.

Le Tambour

SALADES
Composées

CROQUES
au Pain "Moisan"

SANDWICH
Baguette
de Campagne

Café de Flore
PARIS

LE POSH DAY

Did your daddy ever buy you a pony? No, didn't think so, me neither. Well today is the day to make up for that. Call the bank and extend your credit limit because today you are a princess and Paris is your slave to do with what you please. Too much? Well, it is only for a day.

8.00AM
The Parisian Breakfast at Hotel George V

Although normally breakfast should be taken in bed, Le Cinq restaurant in the Hotel George V is definitely worth rising for. I have no idea how a baguette can cost 40€, but then money is no object today and these surrounds are worth every centime.

See page 14

10.00AM
Shop the Golden Triangle

Whether you purchase anything is irrelevant; it's the illusion of money that you need to work with today. Saunter through the triangle d'or, around Avenue Montaigne, Avenue George V and Rue François 1er. I like to pretend I am a Kiribatian princess (see page 124) and swan about trying things on. In this immaculate area you'll find Dior, Chanel, Ferragamo, Dolce & Gabbana, Max Mara, Christian Lacroix, Valentino, Prada and Ungaro. The YSL flagship is there, as is Caron, the famous parfumerie. Spend some time in there – there's nothing like smelling rich, it makes you walk taller.

Around the corner on Avenue George V is Louis Vuitton, Hermès, Givenchy and Kenzo. Keep going up to the Champs-Élysées to Sephora's flagship and freshen up your makeup.

3.00PM
Late lunch at La
Terrasse Montaigne

Shopping this hard can be
exhausting. For the *Sex and the City*
fans out there, you will be familiar
with the Hotel Plaza Athénée. Well,
rest your precious little kitten heels
behind the well-groomed hedges of
La Terrasse Montaigne and have a
champagne and a salade niçoise.

Entrance 27 avenue Montaigne
75008 Paris
Tel: +33 1 53 67 66 00

5.00PM
Dior Institut

Also at the Plaza Athénée you will
find the Dior Institut, where it is
time for a one-hour deep relaxation
massage. It's so hard being a
princess, and no one understands
that better than the fine staff here at
the Institut. Book in advance so you
have it to look forward to.

Hotel Plaza Athénée
25 avenue Montaigne
75008 Paris
Tel: +33 1 53 67 65 35

7.00PM
Le Meurice

Now that you're all floppy and soft,
it's time to go back to your hotel,
run a bath and order room service.
After a five-minute cab ride you'll
be pulling up to the entrance of
Le Meurice, a hotel so luxurious
you might just pass out. Even the
cheapest room is a sensation, so
no need to feel you should book
anything else. Eating a room-service
burger in a bathrobe may not sound
posh, but trust me, it's what all the
princesses are doing these days.

228 rue de Rivoli
75001 Paris
Tel: +33 1 44 58 10 10

LE POSH TIP:

I WENT TO SCHOOL WITH A FIJIAN
PRINCESS. WELL, SHE SAID SHE WAS
A PRINCESS AND WE NEVER
QUESTIONED IT. I MEAN, HOW DO
YOU QUESTION A PRINCESS? SHE
GOT ALL KINDS OF SPECIAL
TREATMENT, WHICH MADE ME THINK,
ANYONE COULD PULL OF THE
PRINCESS SCAM. **WHILE ENJOYING**
YOUR POSH LUNCH/MANICURE/MASSAGE ETC
TRY DROPPING INTO CONVERSATION
YOUR SOVEREIGNTY... ENSURING
YOU CHOOSE A VAGUELY OBSCURE
DESTINATION (E.G. KIRIBATI) THAT
THE FRENCH HAVE NEVER HEARD OF.
'OH WHAT AM I DOING IN PARIS?
MY FATHER, KING MICHI, HAS GRANTED
ME ONE LAST HOLIDAY BEFORE
I RETURN TO MY ISLAND TO MARRY.'

A little further afield . . .

You will have to go a little further north of this map to get to the shops below, but by now the Metro is your BFF, so it shouldn't be any trouble. The area around Tombées du Camion and Café des Deux Moulins is pretty dreary but you have to see the Moulin Rouge at some point, so here are a few things nearby to hold your interest. Maybe you should go at the end of the day so that you can see the windmill on the Moulin Rouge light up?

CAFÉ DES DEUX MOULINS
Sit and sip

15 rue Lepic 75018 Paris
Tel: +33 1 42 54 90 50
Open: Daily 7am–2am
Metro: Blanche

With its fluorescent sign and kitsch interior, it's easy to see why Café des Deux Moulins was featured in *Amélie* as the quintessential Paris café. And the owners aren't shy about reminding us about it either. Audrey Tautou's face is plastered all over the place (clearly there's no such thing as usage fees over here). But a word of warning: for every hopeless romantic customer there's a pervy French gangster-looking dude waiting at the bar to pounce. So try to keep your pretty little doe eyes to yourself. Gee, I sound like your mother now. *Oh, and remember to take a coat. It's chilly out.*

CANAL SAINT-MARTIN

CHEZ PRUNE
Sit and sip

36 rue Beaurepaire
75010 Paris
Tel: *+33 1 42 41 30 47*
Open: *Monday–Saturday*
8am–2am, Sunday 10am–2am
Metro: *République, Jacques*
Bonsergent

If you haven't already picked up the subtle theme of this book, it's all about clothes and shopping. Not so much eating. So on the odd occasion when I do mention a café it's usually because of the location, interior, doable waiters, people-watching et cetera. Chez Prune fits all of these categories. It also fits in the unapologetically French category. When I asked the waiter if they had eggs for breakfast, he replied *'this is Paris, you can have baguette and jam'*. In any other city this might not be a selling point. But here it feels right, and it is the best bread and jam that will ever pass your lips. I think I might use this same technique to promote my book. *This is my book, you can have clothes and shops.*

LOUISE FEUILLÈRE

French knickers

102 rue des Dames
75017 Paris
Tel: +33 1 44 90 96 22
Open: Saturdays 11am–7pm
or by appointment only from
Tuesday to Friday
Closed: Sunday and Monday
and the last Saturday of the month
Metro: Villiers
www.louisefeuillere.com

Made-to-measure lingerie, swimwear, girdles and corsetry for those of you who have just slipped through a wormhole from the eighteenth century.

TOMBÉES DU CAMION

Look at me!

17 rue Joseph de Maistre
75018 Paris
Tel: +33 9 81 21 62 80
Open: Monday–Friday 1pm–8pm,
Saturday & Sunday 11am–8pm
Metro: Abbesses
www.tombeesducamion.com

The difference between crappy junk and chaotic beauty is all in the curating. Tombées du Camion somehow manages to make a shop full of random knick-knacks, vintage toys and button reels into a beautifully arranged collection. Maybe aimed at crafters or collectors of knick-knacks, this shop isn't easy to define. I bought wood block letters spelling out my friend's name and some buttons for 'something I might make one day'. Dolls, plastic whistles, beads, pom poms, boogly eyes – it's a visual feast worth the rummage. Although you shouldn't take the feast thing too literally. I witnessed a kid almost choke to death on a vintage button when I was in there. His mum was too busy to notice that he was turning blue. It's not that she was a bad mother, it's just that the shop is so enticing. Yeah, that'll stand up in court.

Above and overleaf: Tombées du Camion

Le Marais

Le Marais sounds so much nicer than Le Swamp don't you think? Well that's what it could have been called if they didn't drain it back in the ninth century and turn it into a fertile marsh (*marais*) for growing vegetables. The swamp farmers may be long gone but the fertile ground has continued to sprout all kinds of wonderful galleries, cafés, bars and of course shops. From inspirational spaces such as L'Eclaireur to the amazing concept department store Merci, Le Marais is like a fashion biosphere. If not for the pressure to visit the odd landmark to prove to your friends that you really were in Paris, you could easily bunker down and spend your entire time here. In fact, if you take your shopping seriously there are plenty of apartments in the area to rent so you don't really have to leave at all. And it's one of the only shopping areas that is open on a Sunday. But you'll need more than a day to make a dent. I'd allow three to four days to do it properly. And while I'm dishing out advice, make sure you leave room for an afternoon drink (and fumer) at Café Charlot, Mexican at Candelaria, dinner and drinks at the magical Derrière, and coffee and people-watching at Merci. Come to think of it, allow three weeks.

RUE DU TEMPLE

RUE Tsumori Chisa

RUE DES FRANCS-BOURGEO

Claudie Pierlot

RUE DE RIVOLI

Ⓜ SAINT-

ÉCHARLOT

Candelaria

Rose Bakery

VIEILLE DU TEMPLE

BOULEVARD DES FILLES DU CALVAIRE

Ⓜ FILLES DU CALVAIRE

RUE DE TURENNE

L'Éclaireur

BOULEVARD BEAUMARCHAIS

American Vintage

AMERICAN VINTAGE
Affordable chic

10 rue des Francs-Bourgeois
75004 Paris
Tel: +33 1 42 77 98 73
Open: Monday–Saturday
10.30am–7.30pm, Sunday
11am–7.30pm
Metro: Saint-Paul
www.am-vintage.com

Contemporary classics and good quality basics with a slightly misleading name, given that a) it's a French label and; b) it's all brand new.

AQUAVIVE
The Help

119 rue de Turenne
75003 Paris
Tel: +33 1 42 77 93 31
Open: Monday–Saturday
8.30am–7pm
Closed: Sunday
Metro: Filles du Calvaire,
Oberkampf

Aquavive: loosely translates as 'we will dryclean the filthy spills you made on your really expensive dress after a rather messy night out in the Marais'. Drycleaners in the heart of Le Marais, saving us from ourselves.

BA&SH
Cheap and cheerful

22 rue des Francs-Bourgeois
75003 Paris
Tel: +33 1 42 78 55 10
Open: Monday–Saturday
11am–7.30pm, Sunday noon–7pm
Metro: Chemin Vert, Saint-Paul
www.ba-sh.com

I'm not exactly sure how to pronounce this brand. I'm going to go with 'bash'. And bashed is pretty much how I felt after spending five minutes in this store being elbowed by the heaving crowd of perky twenty-somethings. From what I could see through their skinny little legs it looked quite good. Pared-back affordable chic that won't break the bank. Can't say the same for your bones though.

BUBBLE WOOD
The cool gang

4 rue Elzevir
75003 Paris
Tel: +33 1 44 78 03 86
Open: Monday–Saturday
11.30am–7.30pm, Sunday
1pm–7.30pm
Metro: Saint-Paul
www.bubblewood.com

One hundred square metres of mostly Scandinavian cult labels including Wood Wood, Henrik Vibskov and Stine Goya. Popular with local hipsters of the him and her variety. Will the hipster bubble ever burst?

CANDELARIA
Sit and sip

52 rue de Saintonge
75003 Paris
Tel: *+33 1 42 74 41 28*
Open: *Sunday–Wednesday*
noon–11pm, Thursday–Saturday
noon–midnight
Metro: *Saint-Sébastien –*
Froissart, Filles du Calvaire

I can't begin to tell you how much I love it here. As if it is not enough to stumble upon a beautiful Mexican family making authentic tacos right in front of your eyes in an open kitchen, the clientele are all seemingly straight from the pages of a very cool magazine brought to you by the United Colours of Globally Welcoming Paris – every continent is represented under the glow of nasty fluorescent lights. The food is delicious and the staff can't stop smiling. But wait, where are all those hot people going at the back of the café? I'll tell you. They are going out to a cave-like bar in the back for a Ruby Tuesday or a chilli cocktail whose name I can't remember – I just referred to it as 'that spicy little bitch'. That should work with the hot barman with the biceps. Tell him I said hi. Ah, good times.

CLAUDIE PIERLOT
Cheap and cheerful

9 rue des Blancs-Manteaux
75004 Paris
Tel: *+33 1 44 78 03 33*
Open: *Monday–Friday*
10.30am–7pm; Saturday
10.30am–7.30pm; Sunday
1pm–7.30pm
Metro: *Saint-Paul, Hôtel de Ville*
www.claudiepierlot.fr

Someone told me about Claudie
Pierlot before I had ever been.
'Michi,' they said, 'this shop was just
made for you.' And you know what?
It wasn't. It was made for someone
much cuter and better than me.
Someone with a slightly retro, very
simple, French style. Someone who
looks great in a shift dress, a smart
well-tailored pea coat, a sweet pair of
pumps. Someone cool. God damn it.

CORPUS CHRISTI
The cool gang

64 rue Vieille du Temple
75003 Paris
Tel: *+33 1 47 00 45 77*
Open: *Tuesday–Sunday*
11am–7pm
Closed: *Monday*
Metro: *Saint-Paul, Rambuteau*
www.corpuschristi.fr

Thierry Gougenot is one hell of
a jeweller and, I imagine, was a
handful as a kid. The shop looks like
a ship and the jewellery is gothic
with somewhat religious undertones.
You can see that there were pirates
in his childhood – skulls everywhere.
He really did his mum proud. And
she said all that arrr-ing would go
nowhere!

COS
Affordable chic

4 rue des Rosiers 75004 Paris
Tel: *+33 1 44 55 37 70*
Open: *Monday–Saturday*
10am–7pm
Closed: *Sunday*
Metro: *Saint-Paul*
www.cosstores.com

From the clever Swedes who
brought us H&M comes another
retail phenomenon. Sophisticated,
directional fashion that won't break
the bank. I have three different
Cos black dresses, all perfectly cut
and built to last. My mum loves it
too which gave me a great idea. If
you have no money but want to go
shopping in Paris, just tell your
mum how amazing Cos is (no need
to mention they are online and
worldwide), and that she should
definitely pay you to come along and
help her shop. Mother and daughter
Parisian shopping trip? Cos is the
perfect excuse. Not that you need one.

DES PETITS HAUTS

Cheap and cheerful

24 rue de Sévigné
75004 Paris
Tel: *+33 1 48 04 77 25*
Open: *Tuesday–Saturday*
11am–7.30pm, Sunday–Monday
2pm–7.30pm
Metro: *Saint-Paul*
www.despetitshauts.com

From petit things big things grow.
Sisters Katie and Vanessa began
making cute little tops over ten years
ago, and today their Des Petits Hauts
stores are popping up all over Paris.
The stores may be in abundance but
it doesn't feel like a soulless chain.
Affordable chic basics, great prints,
fun printed tees, all with a nice sister
story to match.

DIPTYQUE

Très French

8 rue des Francs-Bourgeois
75003 Paris
Tel: *+33 1 48 04 95 57*
Open: *Sunday–Monday noon–7pm;*
Tuesday–Thursday 11am–7pm;
Friday–Saturday 10.30am–7.30pm
Metro: *Saint-Paul*
www.diptyqueparis.com

Apart from the extra kilos I always
seem to bring home on my derrière,
I also like to come home from Paris
with a booty of beautiful scented
candles from Diptyque. The perfect
gift for those who think you stink for
having a job that involves writing a
book about shopping in Paris – all
will be forgiven when they smell the
Figuier candle you bought them. Ask
for gift wrapping, it's superb.

Florian Denicourt

FLORIAN DENICOURT
Shoes, bags, dog collars

24 rue Charlot
75003 Paris
Tel: +33 1 42 74 88 30
Open: *Tuesday–Saturday*
1pm–8pm
Closed: *Sunday & Monday*
Metro: *Filles du Calvaire,*
Saint-Sébastien – Froissart
www.floriandenicourt.com

I'm the girl on the plane who has
terrible luggage. I am the girl who
carries a canvas shopping tote when
she goes on an overnight trip. The
tote invariably spills its contents
when I try to put it in the overhead
compartment, causing much
embarrassment not only to me, but
also to the poor suity dude who is
sprinkled in knickers and makeup.
So to find luxury French leather
goods shop Florian Denicourt is not
only a revelation, it is also a great
source of envy and disappointment.
You see, I can't afford the simple,
functional and extremely covetable
overnight bags. Every bag is
gorgeous, and I can't afford even the
smallest. But you might be able to, so
I'd say go check it out if you too drop
your knickers on the plane.

GERBE
French knickers

60 rue Vieille du Temple
75003 Paris
Tel: +33 1 42 71 00 50
Open: *Monday–Friday*
11am–7pm, Saturday 10am–7pm
Closed: *Sunday*
Metro: *Saint-Paul*
www.gerbe.com

Terrible name. But if it's stockings
you're after, you're in the right place.
Feet, no feet. Seams, no seams.
Suspenders, knee highs, bodysuits.
Can't gerbe past it.

GLOSS'UP
Pampered Paris

58 rue Charlot 75003 Paris
Tel: +33 6 63 51 20 95
Open: *Tuesday–Saturday*
11am–7pm
Closed: *Sunday & Monday*
Metro: *Filles du Calvaire*
www.gloss-up.com

I couldn't get an appointment at
Gloss'Up last time I was in Paris. I
am not sure if it was because it is an
enormously popular beauty bar and
makeup boutique with a great colour
palette, or just that there seems to
be one lady working there all alone.
Call ahead, she's a busy lass.

ISABEL MARANT ÉTOILE
Affordable chic

47 rue de Saintonge
75003 Paris
Tel: *+33 1 42 78 19 24*
Open: *Monday–Saturday*
10.30am–7.30pm
Closed: *Sunday*
Metro: *Filles du Calvaire*
www.isabelmarant.tm.fr

Isabel Marant's diffusion line is still up there in the 'over my budget' stakes, but not when you look at it side by side with the main line. And, as I am a glass-half-full kinda gal, this is how I choose to see it. Positively affordable and, on a good day, even cheap. Still the same simple, French chic stylings, embroidered shirts, sweet lace tops, cotton gauze smocks and luxe streetwear, but in a wallet-half-full version.

LA PERLE
Sip and sit

78 rue Vieille du Temple
75003 Paris
Tel: *+33 1 42 72 69 93*
Open: *Monday–Friday*
6am–2am, Saturday & Sunday
8am–2am
Metro: *Saint-Paul*

It may not look like anything special, but after a hard day pounding the pavement in Le Marais, La Perle is the perfect place for a well-earned, post-shopping beer. Like most of Le Marais, every man in here looks like they stepped out of Mr Porter and the girls like they dropped from hipster heaven. I don't know exactly why this place is cool, but it makes me want to take up smoking and run off with a waiter every time.

L'ECLAIREUR
Look at me!

40 rue de Sévigné
75004 Paris
Tel: *+33 1 48 87 10 22*
Open: *Monday–Saturday*
11am–7pm
Closed: *Sunday*
Metro: *Saint-Paul*
www.leclaireur.com

I thought I'd be distracted by the 147 televisions playing highbrow video art in this incredible store, but clearly I underestimated my ability to sniff out perfectly pared-back racks of Balenciaga, Comme des Garçons, Christopher Kane, Lanvin and Rick Owens. Designed by Belgian artist Arne Quinze and featuring two tonnes of organic wooden sculpture, this latest offering from the L'Eclaireur family manages to balance high concept art with high fashion. Bloody overachievers.

LOBATO
Shoes, bags, dog collars

6 rue Malher
75004 Paris
Tel: *+33 1 48 82 68 14*
Open: *Monday–Saturday*
11am–7pm
Closed: *Sunday*
Metro: *Saint-Paul*
www.lobato-paris.com

I always get a little anxious about pressing a buzzer to get into a store. What if they look through the glass and decide not to let me in? What if the buzzer is a joke buzzer and it gives me an electric shock? Fortunately for you, I've tested all these potential dangers and I'm happy to report that Lobato is perfectly safe. The only buzz you'll get is from the perfectly edited collection of handbags and footwear by Lanvin, Costume National, Balenciaga, Michel Vivien and Pierre Hardy. Oh and maybe the buzz of your credit card being declined.

LOFT DESIGN BY...
Cheap and cheerful

20 rue des Francs-Bourgeois
75003 Paris
Tel: *+33 1 42 78 62 95*
Open: *Monday–Friday*
10.30am–7.30pm, Saturday
10am–7.30pm
Closed: *Sunday*
Metro: *Saint-Paul*
www.loftdesignby.com

Loft Design By...smells as good as it looks. This French label covers well-fitted contemporary basics, cashmere, accessories and jersey staples. With natural light streaming through the upstairs windows, attentive (and spunky) staff, and the waft of fig candles throughout, it's little wonder this store is a favourite for the modern femme and homme. Gee, that sounds weird? Just trust me, it's lovely.

MATIÈRES À RÉFLEXION

Shoes, bags, dog collars

19 rue de Poitou
75003 Paris
Tel: *+33 1 42 72 16 31*
Open: *Monday–Saturday*
noon–7pm, Sunday 3pm–7pm
Metro: *Filles du Calvaire,*
Saint-Sébastien – Froissart
www.matieresareflexion.com

I once had a fashion student turn a coat into a skirt for me as part of her final assessment. It was part of an eco-friendly, slow fashion project. Matières à Réflexion comes from the same school, so to speak. While it's not for everyone, it is doing the planet a solid without a doubt. It stocks a selection of scarves, sunglasses and jewellery from small independent labels, and is known for its bags which are made from recycled vintage garments. It can be hit and miss. Like my student – she dyed the skirt green and brown because she said I 'reminded her of the Brazilian rainforest'. I was never sure if she meant exciting and busy or just dense and weepy.

MON AMOUR

Paris Vintage

77 rue Charlot 75003 Paris
Tel: *non*
Open: *Monday–Saturday*
noon–7.30pm
Closed: *Sunday*
Metro: *Filles du Calvaire,*
Oberkampf
monamourvintage.blogspot.com

The term 'stylist' is a vague one, I think. A bit like 'lifestyle'. You can have a very average lifestyle, just as you can be a very average stylist. So the phrase 'run by two ex-stylists' really rings alarm bells for me. I mean, if they are no longer in the business, were they any good to begin with? Yes! Emphatically yes! Mon Amour is a lovely vintage shop 'run by two (excellent) ex-stylists'. Good one.

PAUL & JOE SISTER
Cheap and cheerful

56 rue Vieille du Temple
75003 Paris
Tel: +33 1 42 72 42 06
Open: Daily noon–8pm
Metro: Rambuteau, Saint-Paul
www.paulandjoe.com

This is a very pretty shop indeed.
Half of the shop is the Sister brand
of Paul & Joe – a younger diffusion
line from the very sophisticated and
gorgeous French label – and the
other half is menswear. It's full of
light and colour and is just, well,
cheerful. On-trend, fun patterns
everywhere, not expensive – it will
make you smile for sure.

PRETTY BOX
Paris Vintage

46 rue de Saintonge 74003 Paris
Tel: +33 1 48 04 81 71
Open: Tuesday–Saturday
11am–7.30pm
Closed: Sunday & Monday
Metro: Filles du Calvaire
www.prettybox.fr

There are a few things that stand out
here. Number one is the well-edited
vintage clothes, naturally. Christian
Lacroix specs that few could pull
off but which many will try, Hermès
dresses, a fair bit of Chanel, and
mixed in with all that, curiously,
some *Star Wars* paraphernalia. Last
time I was here a lovely lesbian
couple was trying on clothes as
if they were in a montage from a
Disney film. They made me laugh,
commenting on the appropriate name
of the shop – Pretty Box. Indeed!
The other thing that strikes me is
the bear that runs the shop. He may
be quite furry but obviously has
exceptional taste.

Pretty Box

PRINCESSE TAM TAM
French knickers

19 rue Vieille du Temple
75004 Paris
Tel: +33 1 48 04 32 88
Open: Monday 11am–7.30pm,
Tuesday–Saturday 10am–7.30pm
Closed: Sunday
Metro: Saint-Paul
www.princessetamtam.com

Mid-market lingerie brand covering
all your undies needs. Or uncovering,
as the case may be, depending on
your needs. Oh dear, I'll stop.

RETOUCHE
The Help

73 rue Charlot
75003 Paris
Tel: +33 1 42 74 12 44
Metro: Oberkampf

If you happen to lose a few kilos,
need some embroidery done, or need
to get some new buttons made for
an op shop find, this is the place for
you. One of the most highly regarded
destinations for alterations, button
making, and embroidery in Paris.

ROSE BAKERY

Sit and sip

30 rue Debelleyme
75003 Paris
Tel: +33 1 49 96 54 01
Open: Tuesday–Sunday
10am–6pm (kitchen closes at 4pm)
Closed: Monday
Metro: Filles du Calvaire

You'd think the English would think twice before taking on the French in cuisine, but not so for Rose Carrarini. She threw down the gauntlet in 2002 and hasn't looked back (except at the long queues out the door perhaps). Rose Bakery serves delicious and healthy salads, amazing tarts and incredible cakes, all house-made using fresh produce daily. You'd think the fresh bit would be a no-brainer, but in Paris it is actually surprising how much sad lettuce you can see. Rose Bakery is chock-full of stylish visitors and very crunchy lettuce.

> Overleaf: Rose Bakery

SANDRO
Cheap and cheerful

50 rue Vieille du Temple
75004 Paris
Tel: *+33 1 44 59 69 23*
Open: *Daily 10.30am–7.30pm*
Metro: *Rambuteau, Saint-Paul*
www.sandro-paris.com

Did you know that there is a whole
raft of fashion companies who travel
the world to buy clothes, which they
then send to China to get re-made
in a different fabric and with a new
sew-in label and then call their own?
Terrible isn't it? I am going to go out
on a limb here, and say that I reckon
Sandro is one of the shops that they
go to. It's a relatively young company
that started in Le Marais. It's kind
of 80s-inspired with rock influences
like leopard-print miniskirts,
oversized blazers, embellished
t-shirts and ruffle dresses. Not
really my cup of tea but I am always
surprised to find the odd great thing
for me. Until I see the same fab
thing in a million high street shops
back home, that is. Did someone say
influential?

SHINE
Blow it

15 rue de Poitou 75003 Paris
Tel: *+33 1 48 05 80 10*
Open: *Tuesday–Saturday*
10.30am–7.30pm
Closed: *Sunday and Monday*
Metro: *Saint-Sébastien-Froissart,*
Filles du Calvaire
www.shineparis.com

Sometimes a smell can overcome
you. Sometimes you think about a
memory, are thrown into a time gone
by. Sometimes your tummy flips
over when you think you smell an
old boyfriend. Or maybe you gag. In
Shine I am always overcome by the
smell of a holiday I once had with my
family in Vanuatu, kind of a warm
coconut-y smell. But in Vanuatu
there was no Diane von Furstenberg,
no Carven or Helmut Lang. No Marc
Jacobs jellies. No Acne. In Shine
there may be no coconuts, but in
Vanuatu there is no Westwood so I
guess that makes it even.

SURFACE TO AIR
The cool gang

108 rue Vieille du Temple
75003 Paris
Tel: *+33 1 44 61 76 27*
Open: *Monday–Saturday*
11.30am–7.30pm, Sunday
1.30pm–7.30pm
Metro: *Filles du Calvaire,*
Saint-Sébastien – Froissart
www.surfacetoair.com

Here's the thing about Surface to Air: the name is excellent. The name alone says ultra-hip boutique, arty, gallery-type space, unisex streetwear. And you know, it is all those things. They nailed it with one name. There is not much here a girl like me can pull off, but if you are into deconstructed, black, gallery-owner slash artist garb, you're in the right place.

THE KOOPLES

The cool gang

31 rue des Rosiers
75004 Paris
Tel: *+33 1 42 78 74 59*
Open: *Monday 11am–7.30pm;*
Tuesday–Friday 10.30am–7.30pm;
Saturday 10am–7.30pm
Closed: *Sunday*
Metro: *Saint-Paul*
www.thekooples.com

Paris is so mad for this brand, there's
one on every second corner. It's like
their answer to 7/11 but for dressing
androgynous Parisian hipsters. Great
for man-styled workwear, shirts or
for when your boyfriend gets sick of
ladies-only shops.

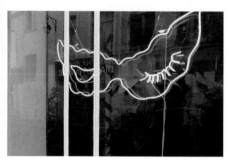

TSUMORI CHISATO
The cool gang / Look at me!

20 rue Barbette
75003 Paris
Tel: *+33 1 42 78 18 88*
Open: *Daily 10.30am–7.30pm*
Metro: *Saint-Paul*
www.tsumorichisato.com

I am from the world of More is More.
There are not that many of us in
this world but I think the numbers
are growing. Right up there with me
in my maximalist world, if not the
leader of the cheer squad, is Tsumori
Chisato. Print on print on pattern
on drawing, it's a mad, mad world in
here. It's not cheap but there is a very
fantastic diffusion line called Cats. It
is for the brave, however, not for the
fraidy-cats.

> *Overleaf: Tsumori Chisato*

LE POSTCARD DAY

Stripy Comme des Garçons t-shirt from Colette?
Check! Eiffel Tower lollypop? Check! There's a reason
Paris is full of clichés. They are all so good. Today is
about getting the postcard moments over and done with
in one big cop-an-Eiffel of a day.

10.00AM
Merci

It may not be on the mainstream
cliché radar, but for me, Merci is
definitely postcard-worthy. The café
has a lovely couch nestled into the
front window – a good place to start
any day. Eat your bread and jam,
have a coffee, look around, and
feel lucky.

111 boulevard Beaumarchais
75003 Paris
Tel: + 33 1 42 77 00 33
Open: Monday–Saturday
10am–7pm
Closed: Sunday
Metro: Sébastien Froissart
www.merci-merci.com

12.00PM
Père Lachaise

Jump on the Metro to Père Lachaise,
the famous cemetery, to see cool
dead people like Chopin, Jim
Morrison, Oscar Wilde, Sarah
Bernhardt, Peter Abelard and
Isadora Duncan. Sure, they may not
be too chatty, but you may never get
this close to such fame again.

Metro: Philippe Auguste,
Gambetta, Pere Lachaise
www.pere-lachaise.com

2.00PM
Café de Flore

It was me. I am the one who ruined it for the rest of you by stealing the menu. Since that crime took place, the waiters have been doubly vigilant about the prized souvenirs. Sorry. Shame they aren't quite as vigilant about the grated carrot salad, but c'est la vie when you're as famous as this place.

See page 172

3.30PM
Colette

After your eggy lunch take a 30-minute stroll over the river and dive into the cult world of Colette. Immaculately dressed mannequins and tables of handpicked designery items make this is a must-see retail landmark. A selection of Paris fashion favourites such as Carven, Cacharel and YSL, as well as hard-to-find sneakers, t-shirts and coffee table books. Think hipster tasting-plate.

See page 46

4.30PM
Seine Boat Ride

Let's face it, more poems have probably been written about the Seine than any other river in the world. Love, hate, murder, suicide but mostly romance. Paying for a ride on such a popular old girl has never felt so good.

en.parisinfo.com/paris-sightseeing/
trips/by-boat

6.00PM
Eiffel Tower

Did you know, that of the 867 million postcards posted each year worldwide, 87% of them have the Eiffel Tower on them? Obviously this means she's quite popular by now, so buy your tickets online at eiffel-tower.com before you go. Stay up when the sun goes down so you can watch the lights come on. And if you're real sucker for postcard moments, get an Eiffel Tower lollipop at the gift shop.

See page 19
Metro: Trocadero,
for the best view of le tour

<u>LE POSTCARD TIP:</u>

SOMEWHERE BETWEEN 1974 AND
1980 EVERY CAFE IN PARIS
DECIDED TO CREATE THE SAME
MENU. QUICHE LORRAINE, QUICHE
FLORENTINE, QUICHE FROMAGE,
QUICHE DU JOUR, QUICHE WITH
GRATED ~~I~~ CARROT SALAD. IF YOU'RE
EGG-INTOLERANT DO NOT FEAR:
THERE'S A SMALL GROUP THAT
MEETS ~~UNDER~~ EVERY SECOND
WEDNESDAY AT 12.45 PM UNDER
THE EIFFEL TOWER FOR GRATED
CARROT SALAD AU NATUREL.

VINTAGE DÉSIR
Paris Vintage

32 rue des Rosiers 75004 Paris
Tel: +33 1 40 27 04 98
Open: Daily 11am–9pm
Metro: Saint-Paul

Vintage and bargain are two words that don't really go together in Paris. Vintage is like platinum and the prices reflect it. Although there are the odd few places, like Vintage Désir, where you can still pick up a vintage bargain (€15 for a dress, €10 for a top). You'll need to dig your way through the crammed racks but there's treasure in there if you're patient. I feel like making a pirate noise now but will refrain.

VALENTINE GAUTHIER
Affordable chic

58 rue Charlot
75003 Paris
Tel: +33 1 48 87 68 40
Open: Monday–Saturday
11am–7.30pm
Closed: Sunday
Metro: Temple, Filles du Calvaire
www.valentinegauthier.com

I have heard Valentine Gauthier referred to as similar to Isabel Marant – contemporary classics, great accessories and very on-trend. I don't actually agree. It seems a bit more roughly made to me, not as polished and definitely not as luxe or expensive. That said, the visual merchandising in the shop is great. It's a friendly space with a chaise and a warmth that is very inviting. And, without wanting to sound roughly made myself, it has nice racks.

YUKIKO
Paris Vintage

97 rue Vieille du Temple
75003 Paris
Tel: +33 1 42 71 13 41
Open: Tuesday–Saturday
11am–1pm, then 2pm–7pm
Closed: Monday and lunchtimes
Metro: Filles du Calvaire
www.yukiko-paris.com

The mannequins in this pretty vintage boutique are lying around posing, saying 'look at me, I'm so hot in my vintage Chanel blazer with my Christian Dior bag coquettishly falling from my slender shoulder'. It may look like a bedroom, but with all that Hermès, it doesn't look like *my* bedroom that's for sure.

Saint-Germain-des-Prés

In the middle of this area is the Benedictine Abbey of Saint-Germain-des-Prés, the oldest church in Paris. This medieval giant dates back to the sixth century and is still immaculate – Descartes is in a tomb in a side chapel, so you know it's really important and well kept. On the left bank of the Seine, this area is famous for its history as an intellectual and artistic hub. You can still feel remnants of good times around here: you can sense the post-WWII cool gang – Picasso, Sartre, de Beauvoir, Beckett and Gainsbourg – whooping it up in the 'hood, no doubt discussing the notion of perpetual despair (ironically, while listening to jazzy-jazz and smoking Gitanes ... yeah, yeah). I found the meaning of life around here, for it was here that Carven and I fell deeply in love. There is nothing better for the human condition than starting the day looking at vibrators in Sonia Rykiel. If you're still in existential crisis, it might help to stop for a glass of rosé at Café de Flore and finish the afternoon off holding a mountain of bags from a successful day on the hunt. In the (similar enough) words of Samuel Johnson, if you are bored in Saint-Germain then you are bored with life.

afé
e Flore

Ⓜ ST-GERMAIN
DES PRÉS

ULEVARD   SAINT-GERMAIN

city
pharmacie

carven

RUE SAINT-SULPICE

UGIRARD

ALEXANDRA SOJFER
Très French

218 boulevard Saint-Germain
75007 Paris
Tel: +33 1 42 22 17 02
Open: Monday–Saturday
9.30am–7pm
Closed: Sunday
Metro: Rue du Bac
www.alexandrasojfer.com

Beautiful parasols, walking canes and leather gloves, like something from a time gone by. It takes a certain type of person to get away with a parasol I think, but if you are that person, this place will be heaven for you. It almost makes you want to slip on a bustle.

CAFÉ DE FLORE
Sit and sip

172 boulevard Saint–Germain
75006 Paris
Tel: + 33 1 45 48 55 26
Open: Daily 7.30am–12.30am
Metro: Saint-Germain-des-Prés
www.cafedeflore.fr

Popular with intellectual types, wealthy women holding tiny dogs, and light-fingered tourists who want to take home the table menu as a souvenir (who me?), Café de Flore is about as French as a snail in a beret smoking with a frog after making love while *Je t'aime* plays in the background. In other words, really, really French. The décor (and some of the dishes) look like they haven't changed in its 120-year history, but that's definitely part of the charm.

CARVEN
Blow it

32–34 rue Saint-Sulpice
75006 Paris
Tel: +33 1 43 54 78 72
Open: Monday–Saturday
10.30am–7.30pm
Closed: Sunday
Metro: Saint-Sulpice,
Sèvres – Babylone
www.carven.fr

I'm going to go out on a limb here and say that if I could only wear one label for the rest of my life this would be it. Except maybe if I lived on a desert island, then I might need to reassess. But until that day comes I'm sticking with the impeccable tailoring and Parisian chic of Carven. I bought a navy tweed jacket one day, then went back a day later to get its friend, Plain Navy Javy. I'm a tragic Carven junkie. I can't go past the cool printed tees, really modern suiting, and fun digital prints mixed with classic-cut wool pants. I hate to use the term 'investment piece' but that's really what you get from this notable French fashion house. Unlike those coconut bikinis, which fell apart after one wash.

CATHERINE B
Paris vintage

1&3 rue Guisarde
75006 Paris
Tel: *+33 1 43 25 64 92*
Open: *Monday–Saturday*
10.30am–7.30pm
Closed: *Sunday*
Metro: *Mabillon,*
Saint-Germain-des-Prés
www.catherine-b.com

Vintage shop owners are usually
quite secretive when it comes to
the sources of their stock. Not
surprisingly, so was Catherine B.
When I asked where they found all
their amazing gold, I was told in
a thick and slightly scary French
accent, 'from people who do not want
it anymore'. But really, who doesn't
'want' vintage Hermès watches and
mint condition Chanel twin sets? I
think there's something dark going
on here. And I like it.

CÉLINE
Blow it

16 rue de Grenelle
75007 Paris
Tel: *+33 1 55 80 14 99*
Open: *Monday–Saturday*
10.30am–7pm
Closed: *Sunday*
Metro: *Saint-Sulpice,*
Sèvres – Babylone
www.celine.com

I wonder what the job description
was for the security guard at Céline?
Really scary man required for really
expensive designer store. Must be
able to blend artfully into a sparse
industrial concrete floor space and
then suddenly appear from nowhere
when customers get too close to
the accessories. Ability to smile not
necessary. If you do find a way past
him, you'll see expensive tailoring,
simple clean lines and sophistication
only money can buy.

CHRISTIAN LOUBOUTIN
Shoes, bags, dog collars

38 rue de Grenelle
75007 Paris
Tel: *+33 1 42 22 33 07*
Open: *Monday–Saturday*
10.30am–7pm
Closed: *Sunday*
Metro: *Rue du Bac*
www.christianlouboutin.com

There's a fine line between stunning and stupid. Christian Louboutin fits this category perfectly. Stunning shoes that cost more than my stupid car. Stupid, rich old men with stunning younger wives. Stupid me for thinking I could walk in a pair of his stunning heels across a stupid shag pile rug. But oh how I want to lie on that rug surrounded by these shoes and roll around in them. Oops, did I just say that out loud?

CITY PHARMA
Pampered Paris

26 rue du Four
75006 Paris
Tel: *+33 1 46 33 20 81*
Open: *Monday–Saturday*
8am–8pm
Closed: *Sunday*
Metro: *Mabillon,*
Saint-Germain-des-Prés

I know what you're thinking, what's a pharmacy doing in a shopping guide? And what's so special about this one? Am I on crack? Or prescription crack? Well, my friends, this place is a goldmine if you're addicted to heavily discounted (really posh) beauty brands such as Darphin, Biotherm, Klorane, Weleda and Roger & Gallet. Dodgy on the outside, desperate skincare junkies on the inside.

LE TINY DAY

Le bon Dieu est dans le détail
– Gustave Flaubert

It's easy in a city like Paris to focus on the big experiences – the big arc, the big churches, the big tower. But not today. Today is about the detail, appreciating the little things that, if unnoticed, would be missed, and when appreciated, are very special indeed.

10.00AM
Jardin du Luxembourg

A big garden full of tiny things. Bartholdi's model Statue of Liberty is here, along with Shetland pony rides and model boats in the lake. Better yet, rent a boat for a lazy half-hour of floating. After all, what better place than Paris to stop and smell the (very manicured) roses?

Metro: Odeon, Cluny La Sorbonne

1.00PM
Tombées du Camion

Jump on the Metro to Blanche and find your way to Tombées du Camion in the 9th to really appreciate how tiny things, when merchandised en masse, can have a big impact.

See page 126

2.00PM
Mon Oncle

French fries are one of my favourite foods. The homemade frites at this tiny Montmartre restaurant are golden and delicious. Not as delicious as all the people in the restaurant, however. I believe there to be a sign on the door saying 'only enter if you're good-looking' – proof that the mirrors above the banquettes were placed there for a reason. Perving.

3 rue Durantin,
75018 Paris
Tel: +33 1 42 51 21 48
Metro: Abbesses

4.00PM
Medecine Douce

Precious little treasures at this very special jewellery shop will have you peering in close for more details. You know you've made it when collaborators include Lacroix, Agnès B and Colette. Medecine Douce works alongside flower-makers, feather-makers, enamellers and embroiderers to create delicate necklaces, cuffs, earrings and bracelets. It's all about the detail here.

10 rue de Marseille,
75010 Paris
Open: *Monday–Saturday*
11am–7pm
Tel: *+33 1 48 03 57 28*
Metro: *République, Jacques*
Bonsergent
www.bijouxmedecinedouce.com

6.00PM
Montmartre for sunset

'Hey, everything looks so tiny from up here!' Take the Funiculaire de Montmartre up the hill, take in the intricacies of the Basilica Sacré-Cœur, then sit and watch the sun set over beautiful Paris.

8.00PM
Candelaria

It's tiny dinner time. Squish into this mini shopfront and down a plate of the best little tacos you'll ever meet. Service comes with a Mexican family of smiles while perched on stools at the kitchen bar. Then duck out the back to finish the night with not-so-small cocktails in the cave-like bar. You may now allow the details to become hazy.

See page 137

LE TINY TIP:

PUT DOWN YOUR TINY CAMERA
AND ENJOY **YOUR** SURROUNDINGS.
MEMORIES ARE BEST CAPTURED
IN THE **MIND**, NOT THE LENS.

ERES
French knickers

4 bis, rue du Cherche-Midi
75006 Paris
Tel: *+33 1 45 44 95 54*
Open: *Monday–Saturday*
10.30am–7pm
Closed: *Sunday*
Metro: *Saint-Sulpice*
www.eresparis.com

Eres was founded in Paris in 1968 and has since established itself as a luxury high-end swimwear and lingerie brand. Nude hues, muted shades, pastels and powdery tones are typical of its collections, even in swimwear. When you're accustomed to fluro surfwear on the beaches of Australia, this really is a very sophisticated breath of fresh air.

IRIS
Shoes, bags, dog collars

28 rue de Grenelle
75007 Paris
Tel: *+33 1 42 22 89 81*
Open: *Monday–Saturday*
10am–7pm
Closed: *Sunday*
Metro: *Saint-Sulpice,*
Sèvres – Babylone
www.irisshoes.com

The difference between good shops and great shops is all in the edit. Iris has taken what could easily be a selection of showy-off brands and made a restrained and well-respected store. I think of it as the shoes I'd like to have under my bed . . . Chloé, Veronique Branquinho, Marc Jacobs, Viktor & Rolf, Jil Sander, Ryan Gosling . . . oh wait he's not a shoe. But you get the picture.

ISABEL MARANT
Blow it

1 rue Jacob 75006 Paris
Tel: +33 1 43 26 04 12
Open: Monday–Saturday
10.30am–7.30pm
Closed: Sunday
Metro: Mabillon,
Saint-Germain-des-Prés
www.isabelmarant.tm.fr

It's no coincidence that tall and skinny stores attract tall and skinny people. Isabel Marant is no exception. Much loved by the French fashion press, this tiny two-level store is constantly packed with beautiful locals and bulging credit cards. The range is small but every garment is perfect – exquisite tailoring, lace details, embroidery. Even though I'm not naive enough to believe these garments are handmade, they feel like one of a kind. The price tags reflect this feeling, sadly.

LES DEUX MAGOTS
Sit and sip

6 Place Saint-Germain-des-Prés
75006 Paris
Tel: *+44 1 45 48 55 25*
Open: *Daily 7.30am–1am*
Metro: *Saint-Germain-des-Prés*
www.lesdeuxmagots.fr

Word on the street is Les Deux
Magots and Café de Flore are fierce
rivals. Both really old, both really
great for people-perving, both really
French. If you don't want to take
sides I suggest you eat at one and
have coffee at the other. Or in the
case of Les Deux Magots, the hot
chocolate (chocolat des Deux
Magots à l'ancienne). Not that it's
a competition.

LE SALON BONAPARTE
Pampered Paris

19 rue Bonaparte
75006 Paris
Tel: *+33 1 43 29 19 19*
Open: *Daily 8am–9pm*
Metro: *Saint-Germain-des-Prés*

As someone who doesn't actually own
a hairbrush, I'm not sure I'm the best
person to be talking about hair. So
when I say this is one of the chicest
hair salons in all of Paris, take it
with a grain of salt. Or a flake of
dandruff. Eww, gross. Sorry. See, you
really shouldn't listen to me on this
subject. I trust my fashion friends
though, and they say go here.

MARLIES DEKKERS
French knickers

10 rue du Cherche-Midi
75006 Paris
Tel: +33 1 42 84 02 40
Open: Tuesday noon–5.30pm,
Wednesday–Saturday 11am–5.30pm
Closed: Sunday & Monday
Metro: Saint-Sulpice
www.marliesdekkers.com

You know how most mannequins are
kind of, well, lifeless and dull? Well
the mannequins in Marlies Dekkers
are totally up for it. I suppose sitting
around in sexed-up avant-garde
lingerie all day will do that to you.

SABBIA ROSA
French knickers

73 rue des Saints-Pères
75006 Paris
Tel: +33 1 45 48 88 37
Open: Monday–Saturday
10am–7pm
Closed: Sunday
Metro: Saint-Germain-des-Prés

If expensive handmade lace knickers that match the colour of macarons appeal to you then Sabbia Rosa will be right up your alley. In fact, it's up the alley of many a cashed-up French model and movie star. Clearly I was not invited to hang out in this particular alley.

SONIA RYKIEL
Blow it

175 boulevard Saint-Germain
75006 Paris
Tel: +33 1 49 54 60 60
Open: Tuesday–Saturday
10.30am–7.30pm
Closed: Sunday & Monday
Metro: Saint-Germain-des-Prés
www.soniarykiel.com

There's a secret room upstairs in Sonia Rykiel that will make you blush. It's past the signature knits and stripes. I'm telling you this so when you do go up there you can act all cool and not pick up a vibrator in the shape of a rubber duck and naively ask the shop assistant, 'What's this?' To be honest, I don't really remember much else about the store after the duck incident but it's Sonia Rykiel and it's Paris, so what could go wrong? Oh that's right, the duck thing.

VANESSA BRUNO
Blow it

25 rue Saint-Sulpice
75006 Paris
Tel: *+33 1 43 54 41 04*
Open: *Monday–Saturday*
10.30am–7.30pm
Closed: *Sunday*
Metro: *Odéon, Saint-Sulpice*
www.vanessabruno.com

Bruno isn't a name I normally
associate with directional or
sophisticated. For me, the name
Bruno conjures up images of a hairy
dude who eats pies for breakfast and
drives a van. However, once you add
the name Vanessa to the mix all
of a sudden the pies and vans are
replaced with silk and sequins.
Not exactly my taste, but then again
I don't have the budget for it anyway.
Might have to stick to the other
Bruno. Ew, that can't be right.

Flea Markets

Everyone will tell you how amazing the markets are in Paris, so there's already a lot of hype to live up to. I'd hate that kind of pressure. I'm so glad I'm not a flea market. Lucky for you, 'most' of the markets are fantastic. And just like most markets around the world, it's ok to bargain in Paris. Personally I'm not linguistically up to it, but if you can speak French, be my guest.

As a rule, you need to dedicate at least half a day to a day to do each properly. If you see something you like, get it then and there. Chances are you'll never find it again. I still lie awake at night thinking of this amazing crocodile suitcase. (If you do happen to find it at Marché aux Puces de la Porte de Vanves can you please bring it back for me? I'll pay you back, I promise.) If you think you'd like to bring something home that won't fit in your crocodile suitcase (like furniture) you can always organise shipping. If you're not in a hurry try FedEx or UPS and ask for freight rates. Many services offer door-to-door delivery — or market-to-door in this case. It can be a bit time-consuming but it'll be worth it in the long haul, when you're sitting back on your chaise longue in five years' time drinking a Brandy Alexander.

LE MARCHÉ DES ENFANTS ROUGES

39 rue de Bretagne 75003 Paris
Open: *Tuesday–Thursday*
8.30am–1pm & 4pm–7.30pm,
Friday & Saturday 8.30am–1pm
& 4pm–8pm, Sunday 8.30am–2pm
Closed: *Monday*
Metro: *Temple*

If you're renting an apartment in the Marais and planning to do some cooking on your trip, Le Marché des Enfants Rouges is a great local market that offers quality produce from all over France. Behind the beautiful (and slightly run-down) arched entry you'll find locals selling all kinds of vegetables, meat, fish, flowers, chocolate, wine and cheese; all delicious and a perfect reason to stop on your way home after a day of shopping. It also serves brunch, coffee and fresh juices on Sundays for those late risers who have been boozing it up across the road at Café Charlot the night before. Not much in the way of clothes (well, none actually) but this is one of my favourite spots to sit and pretend I'm a local while watching the world go by. History lesson: Le Marché des Enfants Rouges was first established in 1615 and was named after the children from the nearby orphanage who dressed in red. As a rule I'm ok with children dressing in red, just not adults. I'll also make an exception for firemen.

LES DOCKS

34 Quai d'Austerlitz
75013 Paris
Open: *Tuesday–Sunday*
10am–6pm
Closed: *Monday*
Metro: *Gare d' Austerlitz,*
Quai de la Gare, Gare de Lyon

It's been described as the 'latest hot spot in Paris'. While I really can't stomach the term hot spot (it makes me think of a venereal disease), Les Docks is definitely a cool new addition to the city. Not quite a market, not exactly a department store, it's more a hybrid of fashion, design and art, and is fast becoming a key centre for emerging creativity in Paris. Inside the architecturally transformed warehouse you'll find galleries, shops, cafés and a très cool (and giant) rooftop nightclub. While I've never been brave enough to go dancing on the roof, the hip young Frenchies seem to love it. Fashion tenants include students of IFM (l'Institut Français de la Mode), Yiqing Yin (she both makes and sells her collections here), Bleu de Paname and a regular stream of pop-up concept stores. Les Docks also hosts exhibitions and shows from more well-known names such as Balenciaga and Comme des Garçons. Near Gare d'Austerlitz, the area is beginning to thrive with the arrival of more cool bars, restaurants and shops. Definitely a 'hot spot' you'll be itching to visit.

> *Overleaf: Marché aux Puces de Saint-Ouen. Above: Le Marché des Enfants Rouges*

FLEA MARKETS

MARCHÉ AUX PUCES DE LA PORTE DE VANVES

Flea market

*Avenues Georges Lafenestre
and Marc Sangnier 75014 Paris*
Open: *Saturday & Sunday
7am–1pm (avenue Marc Sangnier)
and 7am–5pm (avenue Georges
Lafenestre, depending on salesmen)*
Closed: *Monday–Friday*
Metro: *Porte de Vanves*
pucesdevanves.typepad.com

With over 350 dealers, the Puces
de la Porte de Vanves market feels
like one big garage sale. But French.
So it's way cooler. Old ladies selling
even older buttons, cigarette-
smoking Frenchmen playing chess
while ignoring those wanting to buy
their eighteenth-century furniture,
Citroëns backed up to the curb
with boots overflowing with vintage
clothes. Other highlights include
glass and silverware, beautiful old
postcards and photographs, drawings
and paintings, colourful vintage toys,
religious objects, art deco lights, and
even nineteenth-century wedding
dresses if that's your thing. Like all
markets, you can lose hours here, but
at least this one is on the footpath of
a very long, straight street so there's
no getting lost. Keep an eye out for
the 'no photo' signs everywhere.
Stolen goods or just shy, I wonder?

MARCHÉ AUX PUCES DE MONTREUIL

Flea market

*Porte de Montreuil
75020 Paris*
Open: *Saturday–Monday
7am–7.30pm*
Closed: *Tuesday–Friday
(note that many stalls
are also closed Monday)*
Metro: *Porte de Montreuil*

I was told by so many people to go to
this market, but to be honest I don't
get it. It's in a ghetto and I saw a guy
there selling sticks. The people who
recommended it are no longer my
friends. (I was going to delete this
from the book but I don't want you to
make the same mistake I did and end
up spending all your money on dirt
and sticks.)

> Above, opposite and overleaf: Marché aux Puces de la Porte de Vanves

FLEA MARKETS

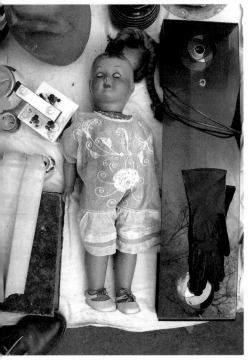

FLEA MARKETS

MARCHÉ AUX PUCES DE SAINT-OUEN
Flea market

Porte de Clignancourt
75018 Paris
Open: *Saturday–Monday*
5am–6pm (approx.)
Closed: *Tuesday–Friday*
Metro: *Porte de Clignancourt*
marchesauxpuces.fr

If you're only going to do one market on your trip, this is the one. A maze of tiny lanes and colourful shacks, Marché aux Puces de Saint-Ouen is one of Europe's most inspirational markets for vintage clothing, antiques and bric-a-brac. You know those people you see on design blogs talking about their annoyingly cool homes? Well this is where they find everything. You could spend a day getting lost meandering through the tiny lanes in search of a piece of Paris to take home. I have a theory that's how some of the stall owners came to be here – after getting lost and deciding that, rather than find their way out, they could just set up camp and make a new life here. Like many of the French, they are quite happy sitting around having a cigarette or dining on a cheese plate rather than worrying about customer service. But once you strike up a conversation they are more than happy to show you their wares, including everything from corsets to miniature French Revolution toy soldiers, colourful outdoor furniture, vintage posters, and even old French construction signs. If you don't find your thing here then maybe you just don't have a thing.

Affordable chic
Agnès B 111, 112, 114
American Vintage 135
Cos 139
Isabel Marant Étoile 146
Valentine Gauthier 167

Blow it
Carven 169, 171, 175
Céline 176
Isabel Marant 182
Shine 158
Sonia Rykiel 85, 169, 188
Vanessa Bruno 189

Cheap and cheerful
BA&SH 135
Claudie Pierlot 132, 138
Etam 96
H&M 91, 92, 101
Loft Design By … 148
Naf Naf 106
Paul & Joe Sister 150
Des Petits Hauts 140
Promod 107
Sandro 158

The cool gang
A.P.C. 111, 114
Acne 67, 69, 71
Bubble Wood 135
Corpus Christi 139
Kitsuné 68, 79
The Kooples 160
Marc Jacobs 67, 82
Stella McCartney Paris 67, 88
Surface to Air 159
Tsumori Chisato 132, 161

French knickers
Chantal Thomass 42, 55
Eres 181
Fifi Chachnil 37, 51
Gerbe 145
Louise Feuillère 126
Marlies Dekkers 187
Princesse Tam Tam 154
Sabbia Rosa 188

The Help
Aquavive 135
Benjamin 38, 41
La Droguerie 102
Mokuba 92, 106
Retouche 154
Last minute gold 7
Annick Goutal 41
Goyard 53
Jean Paul Hévin Chocolatier 57

Look at me!
L'Eclaireur 131, 133, 147
Tombées du Camion 123, 126, 178
Tsumori Chisato 132, 161
Veja Centre Commercial 111,
    112, 116

Pampered Paris
L'Appartement 62
By Terry 95
Carita 42
City Pharma 171, 177
Dior Institut 121
Gloss'Up 145
Manicurist 19
Le Salon Bonaparte 186
Sephora 91, 92, 109, 120
Shiseido by Serge Lutens 88
La Sultane de Saba 91, 102

Paris vintage
Catherine B 176
Didier Ludot 67, 68, 71
Episode 95
Free'P'Star 91, 92, 96
Kiliwatch 92, 101
Mon Amour 149
Pretty Box 150
Room Service 109
Vintage Désir 167
Yukiko 167

Shoes, bags, dog collars
Christian Louboutin 95, 170, 177
Florian Denicourt 145
Gabrielle Geppert 73
Iris 181
Lobato 147
Matières à Réflexion 149
Pierre Hardy 87
Repetto 37, 39, 64

Sit and sip
Café des Deux Moulins 123
Café de Flore 165, 169, 171,
    172, 186
Candelaria 131, 133, 137, 179
Chez Prune 111, 113, 125
Les Deux Magots 186
Maxim's 37, 38, 62
La Perle 146
Rose Bakery 133, 155

Très French
Alexandra Sojfer 172
Les Arts Décoratifs 80
Colette 39, 46, 165
Diptyque 140
Hôtel Costes 37, 39, 55, 57
Ladurée 59
Maison Fabre 69, 80
Petit Bateau 64

INDEX

A

A.P.C. 111, 114
Above Hôtel de Ville 91–109
accommodation
  apartments 12–13, 131
  hotels 14–15
Acne 67, 69, 71
Affordable chic 6
  Agnès B 111, 112, 114
  American Vintage 135
  Cos 139
  Isabel Marant Étoile 146
  Valentine Gauthier 167
Agnès B 111, 112, 114
Airbnb apartments 13
airport, train to 16
Alexandra Sojfer 172
American Vintage 135
Annick Goutal 41
apartments
  Airbnb apartments 13
  Herouet Apartment 13
  in Le Marais 131
  Paris Attitude apartments 13
  3 Rooms Alaïa apartments 12
L'Appartement 62
Aquavive 135
arrival in Paris 16
arrondissements 2–3, 4
Artazat 98
Les Arts Décoratifs 80
autumn in Paris 9

B

BA&SH 135
bags see Shoes, bags, dog collars
bargaining 191
Basilica Sacré-Coeur 179
beach (pretend)
  Paris Plage 99
Benjamin 38, 41
bike-riding 25, 54
Blow it 6
  Carven 169, 171, 175
  Céline 176
  Isabel Marant 182
  Shine 158
  Sonia Rykiel 85, 169, 188
  Vanessa Bruno 189

boat rides 165
Le Bon Marché 29, 30, 170
bookstores
  Artazat 98
  7L Librairie 84
Bubble Wood 135
buses 25
By Terry 95

C

Café Charlot 131, 192
Café de Flore 165, 169, 171, 172, 186
Café des Deux Moulins 123
Canal Saint-Martin 98, 110–29
Candelaria 131, 133, 137, 179
Carita 42
Carven 169, 171, 175
Catherine B 176
Céline 176
cemetery
  Père Lachaise 164
Centre Pompidou 92
Chantal Thomass 42, 55
Le Châteaubriand restaurant 17
Cheap and cheerful 6
  BA&SH 135
  Claudie Pierlot 132, 138
  Etam 96 H&M 91, 92, 101
  Loft Design By... 148
  Naf Naf 106
  Paul & Joe Sister 150
  Des Petits Hauts 140
  Promod 107 Sandro 158
Chez Prune 111, 113, 125
Christian Louboutin 95, 170, 177
City Pharma 171, 177
Claudie Pierlot 132, 138
Colette 39, 46, 165
The cool gang 6
  A.P.C. 111, 114
  Acne 67, 69, 71
  Bubble Wood 135
  Corpus Christi 139
  Kitsuné 68, 79
  The Kooples 160
  Marc Jacobs 67, 82
  Stella McCartney Paris 67, 88
  Surface to Air 159
  Tsumori Chisato 132, 161
Corpus Christi 139
Cos 139
The Crazy Horse 85
currency 22

D

department stores
  Le Bon Marché 29, 30, 170
  Galeries Lafayette 22, 30, 99
  Merci 22, 131, 164
  Printemps 22, 35
Derrière restaurant 17, 85, 131
Les Deux Magots 186
Didier Ludot 67, 68, 71
dinner reservations 17
Dior Institut 121
Diptyque 140
Les Docks 192
La Droguerie 102

E

L'Eclaireur 131, 133, 147
Eiffel Tower 165
tickets 19
Episode 95
Eres 181
Etam 96

F

fashion shows
  Les Docks 192
  Galeries Lafayette 99
fashion weeks 9
Fifi Chachnil 37, 51
flea markets
  bargaining 191
  Les Docks 192
  Le Marché des Enfants Rouges 192
  Marché aux Puces de Montreuil 196
  Marché aux Puces de la Porte de Vanves
    191, 196
  Marché aux Puces de Saint-Ouen 201
Florian Denicourt 145
forwarding services 23, 191
Four Seasons George V Paris 14, 120
Le Free Day 98–100
Free'P'Star 91, 92, 96
French knickers 7
  Chantal Thomass 42, 55
  Eres 181
  Fifi Chachnil 37, 51
  Gerbe 145
  Louise Feuillère 126
  Marlies Dekkers 187
  Princesse Tam Tam 154
  Sabbia Rosa 188
Funiculaire de Montmartre 179

G

G7 Taxi Service 16
Gabrielle Geppert 73
Galeries Lafayette 22, 30, 99
Gerbe 145
getting around 24–5, 54, 165
Gloss'Up 145
Golden Triangle 120
Le Good Times Day 84–6
Goyard 53

H

H&M 91, 92, 101
The Help 7
  Aquavive 135
  Benjamin 38, 41
  La Droguerie 102
  Mokuba 92, 106
  Retouche 154
Herouet Apartment 13
hotels
  Four Seasons George V Paris 14, 120
  Hôtel Le Bellechasse 15
  Hôtel Costes 37, 39, 55, 57
  Hôtel Le Crayon 14
  Mama Shelter 15 Le Meurice 121

I

Iris 181
Isabel Marant 182
Isabel Marant Étoile 146

J

Jardin du Luxembourg 178
Jean Paul Hévin Chocolatier 57

K

Kiliwatch 92, 101
Kitsuné 68, 79
The Kooples 160

L

Ladurée 59
Last minute gold 7
  Annick Goutal 41
  Goyard 53
  Jean Paul Hévin Chocolatier 57
Lobato 147
Loft Design By … 148
Look at me!
  7 L'Eclaireur 131, 133, 147
  Tombées du Camion 123, 126, 178
  Tsumori Chisato 132, 161

Veja Centre Commercial 111, 112, 116
Louise Feuillère 126
Louvre museum 69, 99
Le Lovers Day 54–6

M
Maison Fabre 69, 80
Mama Shelter 15
Manicurist 19
Le Marais 3, 12, 13, 19, 21, 131–67
Marc Jacobs 67, 82
Le Marché des Enfants Rouges 192
Marché aux Puces de Montreuil 196
Marché aux Puces de la Porte deVanves
    191, 196
Marché aux Puces de Saint-Ouen 201
Marché Raspail 99
markets
    Marché Raspail 99
    see also flea markets
Marlies Dekkers 187
Matières à Réflexion 149
Maxim's 37, 38, 62
Medecine Douce 179
Merci 22, 131, 164
Metro (underground) 24
Le Meurice 121
Mokuba 92, 106
Mon Amour 149
Mon Oncle 179
Montmartre at sunset 179
Moulin Rouge 123

N
Naf Naf 106

O
online shopping 23
opening hours 21

P
packing for Paris 10–11
Palais Royal and surrounds 3, 66–89
Palais de Tokyo 85
Pampered Paris 7
    L'Appartement 62
    By Terry 95
    Carita 42
    City Pharma 171, 177
    Dior Institut 121
    Gloss'Up 145
    Manicurist 19
    Le Salon Bonaparte 186

Sephora 91, 92, 109, 120
Shiseido by Serge Lutens 88
La Sultane de Saba 91, 102
Paris
    accommodation 12–15
    arrival 16
    arrondissements 2–3, 4
    dinner reservations 17
    fashion weeks 9
    getting around 24–5, 54, 165
    packing for 10–11
    restaurant reservations 17
    scams 100
    when to go 8–9
    see also days off; shopping
Paris Attitude apartments 13
Paris Plage 99
Paris vintage
    Catherine B 176
    Didier Ludot 67, 68, 71
    Episode 95
    Free'P'Star 91, 92, 96
    Kiliwatch 92, 101
    Mon Amour 149
    Pretty Box 150
    Room Service 109
    Vintage Désir 167
    Yukiko 167
Paul & Joe Sister 150
Père Lachaise cemetery 164
Les Perfect Days
    Le Free Day 98–100
    Le Good Times Day 84–6
    Le Lovers Day 54–6
    Le Posh Day 120–2
    Le Postcard Day 164–6
    Le Tiny Day 178–80
La Perle 146
Petit Bateau 64
La Petite Robe Noir 71
Des Petits Hauts 140
Pierre Hardy 87
Pink Flamingo 113
Le Planning 8–19
Le Pont Des Arts 54
Le Posh Day 120–2
Le Postcard day 164–6
Pretty Box 150
Princesse Tam Tam 154
Printemps 22, 35
Promod 107

Q
quiches 166

R
Repetto 37, 39, 64
restaurants
    Le Châteaubriand restaurant 17
    Derrière restaurant 17, 85, 131
    Mon Oncle 179
    reservations 17
    Restaurant le Meurice 84
    La Terrasse Montaigne 121
    Verjus bar/restaurant 79
Retouche 154
Room Service 109
Rose Bakery 133, 155

S
Sabbia Rosa 188
Saint-Germain-des-Prés 3, 12, 15, 169–89
sales 21
Le Salon Bonaparte 186
Sandro 158
scams 100
Seine Boat Ride 165
Sephora 91, 92, 109, 120
7L Librairie 84
Shine 158
shipping things back 23, 191
Shiseido by Serge Lutens 88
Shoes, bags, dog collars 6
    Christian Louboutin 95, 170, 177
    Florian Denicourt 145
    Gabrielle Geppert 73
    Iris 181 Lobato 147
    Matières à Réflexion 149
    Pierre Hardy 87
    Repetto 37, 39, 64
shopping
    bargaining 191
    currency 22
    fashion weeks 9
    forwarding services 23, 191
    Golden Triangle 120
    online 23
    opening hours 21
    sales 21
    Sundays 19, 21, 131
    VAT 22, 29
shopping categories 6–7
sit and sip 7
    Café des Deux Moulins 123
    Café de Flore 165, 169, 171, 172, 186

Candelaria 131, 133, 137, 179
Chez Prune 111, 113, 125
Les Deux Magots 186
Maxim's 37, 38, 62
La Perle 146
Rose Bakery 133, 155
Sonia Rykiel 85, 169, 188
spring in Paris 8
Stella McCartney Paris 67, 88
La Sultane de Saba 91, 102
summer in Paris 8
Sunday shopping 19, 21, 131
Surface to Air 159

T
taxis 16, 25
La Terrasse Montaigne 121
3 Rooms Alaïa apartments 12
Le Tiny Day 178–80
Tombées du Camion 123, 126, 178
train to airport 16
Très French 6
    Alexandra Sojfer 172
    Les Arts Décoratifs 80
    Colette 39, 46, 165
    Diptyque 140
    Hôtel Costes 37, 39, 55, 57
    Ladurée 59
    Maison Fabre 69, 80
    Petit Bateau 64
Tsumori Chisato 132, 161
Tuileries Gardens and surrounds 5, 36–65

U
underground (Metro) 24

V
Valentine Gauthier 167
Vanessa Bruno 189
VAT 22, 29
Veja Centre Commercial 111, 112, 116
Verjus bar/restaurant 79
vintage see Paris vintage
Vintage Désir 167

W
walking 25
winter in Paris 9, 10

Y
Yukiko 167

VIKING

Published by the Penguin Group
Penguin Group (Australia)
707 Collins Street, Melbourne, Victoria 3008, Australia
(a division of Pearson Australia Group Pty Ltd)
Penguin Group (USA) Inc.
375 Hudson Street, New York, New York 10014, USA
Penguin Group (Canada)
90 Eglinton Avenue East, Suite 700, Toronto, Canada ON M4P 2Y3
(a division of Pearson Penguin Canada Inc.)
Penguin Books Ltd
80 Strand, London WC2R 0RL England
Penguin Ireland
25 St Stephen's Green, Dublin 2, Ireland
(a division of Penguin Books Ltd)
Penguin Books India Pvt Ltd
11 Community Centre, Panchsheel Park, New Delhi 110 017, India
Penguin Group (NZ)
67 Apollo Drive, Rosedale, Auckland 0632, New Zealand
(a division of Pearson New Zealand Ltd)
Penguin Books (South Africa) (Pty) Ltd
Rosebank Office Park, Block D, 181 Jan Smuts Avenue, Parktown North, Johannesburg 2196, South Africa
Penguin (Beijing) Ltd
7F, Tower B, Jiaming Center, 27 East Third Ring Road North, Chaoyang District, Beijing 100020, China

Penguin Books Ltd, Registered Offices: 80 Strand, London WC2R 0RL, England

First published by Penguin Group (Australia), 2013

1 3 5 7 9 10 8 6 4 2

Text and photography © Chloe Quigley & Daniel Pollock 2013
Illustrations © Kat Macleod 2013

The moral right of the authors has been asserted

Cover design and illustration by Kat Macleod, Ortolan
Illustrations by Kat Macleod, Ortolan
Text design by Allison Colpoys
Colour reproduction by Splitting Image Colour Studio Pty Ltd, Clayton, Victoria
Printed and bound in China by 1010 Printing International Limited

National Library of Australia
Cataloguing-in-Publication data:
Quigley, Chloe, author.
Le shop guide: The best of Paris for the fashion traveller / by Chloe Quigley and Daniel Pollock;
illustrations by Kat Macleod; design by Allison Colpoys.
9780670076680 (paperback)
Shopping--France--Paris--Guidebooks.
Paris (France)--Guidebooks.
Paris (France)--Social life and customs.
Pollock, Daniel, author.
Macleod, Kat, illustrator.
Colpoys, Allison, designer.
381.102544361

penguin.com.au

* Thanks to the following lovely stores for providing images while I was too busy shopping:
Galeries Lafayette: 30; Le Bon Marché: 28, 30, 31; Printemps: 32–33, 34; Colette: 46, 47, 48–49; Acne: 70, 71;
Maison Fabre: 80, 81; Marc Jacobs: 82, 83; La Sultane de Saba: 102, 103; Surface to Air: 159;
Tsumori Chisato: 161, 162–163; Carven: 174, 175. Copyright for these images is retained by the individual stores.

* Photograph on page 30 kindly supplied by Getty Images.